Unexpected Consequences

What a joy to narrate this book! One of the things I enjoyed the most was the authentic relationship between the girlfriends. It didn't try to emulate the typical caricatures that have been so overdone; but instead offered something fresh and unique. I also really enjoyed reading about family dynamics within Black aristocratic culture, which is something I don't know much about. There's so much to unpack here! This is a great book for a book club, podcast or discussion group.
—Kimberly Yvonne Steele

I could not put this novel down. All of my emotions were triggered. These ladies are a mess!!!
—Terri Murphy

BJ is honest, poignant, and hilarious in her writing. This is a must read. Sit back with a cup or a glass of whatever and enjoy.
—Marjorie Frazier Shaw

Fun read and thought provoking.
—Dottie Frazier

This book made me laugh out loud, made me cry and made me think. Thank you BJ.
—Austin Pope

WTTF and Unexpected Consequences

WTTF and Unexpected Consequences

Sometimes, Low-Vibing Spirits Will Make You Scream, "What the Total F*ck Is Really Going On?"

BJ Holmes

Balanced Crown Productions, LLC
Smoke Rise, Georgia

This is a work of fiction. Names, characters, businesses, places, and events are either the products of the author's imagination or are used in a fictitious manner. Any resemblance to actual persons, living or dead, or actual events is purely coincidental.

Copyright © 2022 by Belinda Holmes

All rights reserved. No part of this book may be reproduced or transmitted in any form or by any means, electronic or mechanical, including photocopying, recording, or any information storage and retrieval system, without permission in writing from the author.

ISBN: 978-1-7378740-1-0 - Hardcover
ISBN: 978-1-7378740-0-3 - Paperback
eISBN: 978-1-7378740-4-1 - eBook

Printed in the United States of America   070822

∞This paper meets the requirements of ANSI/NISO Z39.48-1992 (Permanence of Paper)

Uncle Nearest 1856 is the trademark of Uncle Nearest Premium Whiskey and is wholly and independently owned by Uncle Nearest, Inc.
Development Editor and Coach: Dr. M. Wendy Hennequin
Literary Mentor: Dr. William Harold Hardy

To my awesome daddy, George Odis Holmes Sr. Thank you for believing, loving, and supporting me. To my late brother, Little George; late nephew, Angel Beverly; and to all of my ancestors that survived. Y'all grant me the blessing of seeing the morning sun.

Thanks to Daddy
*I've mastered the gift of walking away, not giving a f*ck, and never looking back. The sun IS brighter when you step away from shady people, places, and things.*
Stay beautiful.
—BJ Holmes

PROLOGUE: LET'S TRAVEL TO SOULSVILLE

Joy

I am Joy, a wise spirit beyond my years and somewhat of a rebel with a cause. Welcome to my world. Like it or leave it, I don't give a hoot what people think of how I live my life. Married six times, so what? Regardless, I continue to believe in love. I live unapologetically, love myself first, own my happiness, and am brutally honest to a fault. I encourage everyone to do the same and to fight, even if it means fighting to save yourself from your lower self.

Allow me to use your third eye to visualize my life's journey. Yes, life is a wonderful journey that starts at conception and ends with death of the body. During your travels, sometimes you will have riding partners. Mine are Gypsy and Michael, the best friends a girl could ask for. Gypsy, a calming, loyal, maternal force, is loving and caring when it comes to her family and true friends. Michael, young, sweet, and a real go-getter, is committed to a narcissistic, cheating, and abusive husband, Darren. With the help of Gypsy and myself, Michael learns the importance of self-love.

But back to my six husbands—they do not deserve the use of proper names. So, moving forward I will just refer to them as Mess Numbers One through Six.

If you enjoy drama, thrillers, suspense, and humor, my story is the one for you.

CHAPTER 1

BULLY WITH NO SHAME

Joy

Jesus, take the wheel! This guy sitting next to me in the team meeting is fine as hell. I wonder what he would do if I reached under the table and rubbed his thigh. Girl, stop.

My manager, Karen, sat on the other side of the table looking like she just ate something bitter. During our break, I asked her what was wrong. Reaching for my hand, she said, "Walk with me back to my office."

When we reached her office, she closed the door and cried like she'd had a death in the family. Wiping her eyes, she told me her manager said the report she had been working on for the last month was garbage, and he tossed it.

I reached my arms out for a supportive hug, and she whispered, "He is such a bully. He constantly puts me down, and he has the nerve to scream at me."

Pushing her away and looking into tear-filled eyes, I said, "Karen, stand up for yourself. Do not cower behind the fear of losing your job. Go to HR and tell them what's going on!"

By the time we got back to the conference room, her manager was handing out his presentation. When I looked at it, my mouth dropped and my eyes went straight to Karen.

Well, I'll be damned. That bully-bastard is going to present Karen's report—the report that he said was garbage, the report he screamed at her about, the report that made her cry—as his own.

When it was time for him to present, I took pleasure in watching him stumble through "his" report like a kid trying to recite someone else's Easter speech and was proud of Karen for not helping his bully ass out.

After the meeting, I followed Karen back to her office. She sat at her desk, dropped her head, and sobbed. Seeing her broken took me back to my childhood, how I slew a kindergarten bully with the truth.

CHAPTER 2

THE BULLY SLAYER

Joy

My dad worked at night, and my mom taught school during the day, so Daddy was often my babysitter. When he had to work overtime, Daddy would leave me with our neighbor Mrs. Thomas at her café, the Red Chicken. When I was at the café, I loved sitting in the tan booth next to the large window with the picture of a chicken in red-painted heels. Why? So I could see what grown folks did when they thought no one was looking.

Sitting by the window, I saw this lady get into a blue car that was parked across the street and leave with a man from my church wearing a black hat. When they came back, they sat in the car and talked for a long time.

Out of nowhere, this tall man holding a large brown belt walked up to the car, opened the door, and pulled the lady out by her arm. He whooped her butt with that belt, like she'd stolen something. The man from church drove off so fast, his hat flew out the window and his tires made a big cloud of black smoke.

Hearing the commotion, Mr. and Mrs. Thomas ran to the window next to my booth. Shaking her head and resting both hands on her massive hips, Mrs. Thomas said, "It is a cotton-picking shame how Deacon Korn is beating his wife, right in the damn street. I'm not sure why he is so upset. I know for a *fact* he has two young girls at church in the family way, and he has been sleeping with the pastor's wife for years!"

Throwing his hands up and running to the door, Mr. Thomas screamed, "Lord, the po' child done ran from under her wig."

Watching with my five-year-old eyes, I could not figure out why Mrs. Korn would get a beating just because she shared a ride with the nice man in the big hat from church.

When Daddy picked me up, he asked about my day. I told him what happened to the lady. Then I asked him, "What's 'in the family way' mean?"

He didn't answer. Instead, he asked me if I was excited about starting kindergarten next week.

Slowly, I said, "I think so." I wanted to say, "No, I enjoyed sitting by the café window."

The next week, Daddy drove me to kindergarten. When he parked and I saw the kids playing, I thought, *Maybe I could put up with this for a minute.* Just as I thought that, I saw Deacon Korn get out of his car with a little boy wearing blue shorts and white shoes. I found out later it was his son, Junior Korn.

We called the kindergarten teacher "Teacher." She was a heavy-set lady with thick glasses, and I can never remember her smiling.

The classroom seemed so large, and the restroom was in the front of the class. You can only imagine the pressure of having to get up and walk across the room to use the restroom. By the second day, I mastered the art of holding my business until recess.

All the letters of the alphabet I had been working on were around the walls. Coming from a family of teachers, they expected someone to have started working with me before coming to kindergarten.

On my second day, Junior Korn told me I was ugly and kicked my foot so hard, he left dirt on the new socks Daddy bought me. When Teacher caught me punching him in the eye, she made me come to her desk. "So, Miss Joy, I see you felt like fighting today."

I tried to explain what had happened, but she said, "Little lady, you were told if you get caught hitting, you will get a spanking. Stop talking back. I know what I saw."

Wait, I did not sign up for this! My daddy doesn't spank me, so I know damn well you are not going to, I thought, but dared not to say it. Then she told me to turn my butt to the class, but I stood still. Each time she tried to turn me around, I resisted. *If you are going to spank me, I want the class to see I did not cry.*

So, she gave up and just started whaling on my butt while I faced the class. During my spanking, I looked at laughing Junior Korn straight in his eyes, thinking how I was going to get back at him for getting me into trouble.

When she finished, I slowly turned around and just stared at Teacher. I guess she did not realize I was a grown-up in a five-year-old's body. I could take my licks, I could look you in the eye, and I could think.

For the rest of the day, I was not thinking about no ABCs. All I was thinking about was teaching Junior Korn and Teacher a lesson about bullying and hitting me.

During lunch, when Junior Korn made fun of me getting a spanking, I said, "Junior, I saw your daddy beat your mama's butt when she was with the man from church, and she 'ran from under her wig.'"

I repeated what Mrs. Thomas had said about his daddy. Everyone laughed but Junior. He left his lunch, told me he hated me, and ran to the restroom. From that day, he never bullied me or any of the other kids again.

Now to teach Teacher a lesson.

Later that afternoon, I saw her go into the small restroom that was in front of the class. I waited a couple of minutes. Then, I just pretended I had to use the restroom, too, knowing all the while that she was in there. I opened the door for the whole class to see.

There she sat, with her large drawers around her ankles, leaning forward, getting ready to wipe her butt. She looked around with those thick glasses hanging on her nose and saw me there holding the door wide open. Teacher reached over and just snatched the door out of my hand. You could hear the slam throughout the tiny classroom.

Before she came out, I ran back to my seat, knowing damn well I was in big trouble.

When she finally walked out, she had to face a classroom of laughing kids. As soon as she got herself together, she called my dad to pick me up. She stood by the side door next to the playground until she saw him pull up. Grabbing me by the arm, she met him at the car and—with her head moving and wig shaking—she told him about the restroom door and my fight with Junior, but she said nothing about spanking me.

All Daddy said was, "I will handle it."

After we got in the car, he looked me straight in the eye. "Now you tell me what happened."

So, I told my dad why I punched Junior Korn and why I opened the restroom door. He seemed upset with me about opening the door, but said nothing about punching Junior.

After we talked, he pulled out from school and we rode in silence. Before we made it home, I started to cry like a baby, saying how sorry I was for everything, and, being my dad, he pulled my ponytail and reassured me all was good. To make me feel better, we went to get some ice cream, and as punishment, I had to go to bed as soon as we got home.

After my fight with Junior, his parents stopped speaking to my parents. I never understood why, the fight was between Junior and me.

CHAPTER 3

GIRL, STOP AND COME ON

Joy

After the crazy meeting with Karen's boss, I received an email from one of my book-club girls telling the crew about a free jazz concert at Centennial Park. As of July, we have thrown six parties, gone on two out-of-town trips, attended two concerts, and have only read one book.

Karen had been driving me crazy crying about her bully-ass boss, and I decided I had enough of dealing with low-vibing people, so I took a half-day. To keep your energy high, remember self-love, self-knowing, and self-preservation foremost are necessities. People must be ready for high energy, but until then, leave them to God.

I jumped into my brand-new, little red convertible, dropped the top, and hauled ass.

The traffic in Atlanta was butt-crazy. Just my luck. The light on Ponce and Highland was out again, and I wasn't sure where some of these folks got their licenses. When the light is out, you treat it like a four-way stop; you don't just fly through the intersection! In Atlanta, you need to drive for you, the other guy, *and* the fool behind you.

No matter how crazy it is, I love this city. I've always said if your relationship is not solid when you move to Atlanta, it will break down within six months. I should know, considering I divorced Mess Number One six months after landing in the Atlanta airport.

I confess, I broke up at least two "happy" homes. I had to cool my heels after one of my insane, married boyfriends tried to beat the crazy out of me. It took three months to get my arm out of the stupid sling, and two months to get my leg out of that funky brace.

Damn, how did I get two broken bones in one fight?

I should have made it clear about my intentions. Boys kill me, thinking you want them for keeps. They are just something to do until the next episode. He should have known he could play, but he must stay. Stay home with "Wifey."

Oh, well. I mended all—mind, body, and spirit. Lesson learned.

Lucky me, I found a parking spot close to the park and a suitable spot for me to slip on my halter top. Funny, the last time I did a quick change in the car, I took off my top and the collar caught on my earring. It took me ten minutes to get straightened out, showing my "ta-tas" the entire time. Wouldn't you know it, I got busted by this fine piece of work smiling like a damn fool. He had the freaking nerve to lean over in the car and ask me if I needed some help. He waited for me to get out of the car and asked me out.

I dated him for over a year. It was a ball.

After I got the roof up, I grabbed the cooler with my

special lemonade. *I better hurry and beat the crowd,* I thought. *Remember, this is a "free" concert.*

When I got to the gate, the lady cop asked me to open my bag. *Snap, they are checking bags.* If the security knew how "special" this lemonade was, they would lock me up. She searched my bag like she was looking for a bomb. I guess she did not find what she was looking for, because she looked up at me and told me to have a good time.

When I walked into the concert, I took note of all the people moving around, eating, and just enjoying themselves. *These men are yummy, and the ladies are gorgeous.* That's right, I checked them both out. I needed to keep an eye on the hunters *and* the prey. You know the Atlanta ladies will improve the trap game hourly. I think they picked up momentum back in the '80s starting with fake eye color, then in the '90s with the weave, and the 2000s with their fake breasts and butts. Back in the day, redbones were considered different. Now I wondered if my real hair and eyes looked fake.

Look at this young queen with the six-pack! I am sure some would ask why she's smiling and hugging up with the brother who has bad feet and no pack. She knows what is important. Forget the looks—if he treats you like a queen, then he is your Prince Charlie. Handle your business, sweetie.

The wind was blowing the sweet smell of barbecue. I knew better than to venture down that path. The last time I ate at one of these joints, I had to find a portable outhouse in such a hurry, I almost didn't make it. Thank God for strong glutes and long legs.

Just as I passed the wing stand, someone shouted out, "Hey, pretty Joy!"

I thought to myself, *Now, there is only one person that calls me that.* I turned around and, Lord, I could not believe my eyes. It was one of my old, hot flames, Gus. He looked like he had lost a ton of weight. *Lord, I hope this was a planned weight loss.*

Gus motioned for me to come over. As I got closer, he ran over and gave me a big hug and whispered in my ear, "Baby, it is so good to see you."

Yes, this was my old friend Gus. I could feel his blessing pressing on my thigh.

He pulled back, looked at me, and said, "You look great."

After I got myself together, I returned the compliment. "No, *you* look great. What is going on with you?"

He replied, "Nothing much. Just started eating right and running five miles daily around Stone Mountain."

I told him it was really paying off.

Looking at me like I was a steak with all the sides, he said, "Let's catch up over dinner."

"Sure," I said. Of course, I was game, but I needed to remember why I kicked him to the curb. No need to let the same dog bite me twice. Even if it is a poodle, the bite is the same.

Before parting ways, he hugged and kissed me right on the freaking mouth. I did not turn away. We made dinner plans for next week, and I continued my journey.

I needed to hurry. The first act was over, and I wasn't even seated yet. I couldn't see the girls, so I decided I'd better call. I did not have the energy to wander around in the hot sun, and you know Black folk have a problem with moving their legs in a crowd. Thank God for cell phones.

I checked my last dialed number: Gypsy.

Let me tell you about Ms. Gypsy. She is six feet one, blonde (brown roots), and knows she is fine. But she is very humble with her beauty and has a heart of gold.

On the first ring, Gypsy answered. "We are close to the right speaker. Hurry up with your never-on-time behind, and stop talking to every man in the park!"

Pulling the phone from my ear, I wondered how she knew what I was up to. As soon as I hung up, she called back. "Since you are late, please get a bag of ice."

Good thing I called. If they would have waited until I got close to my seat, they would have been a bunch of hot, mad, *and* iceless sistas.

While looking for ice, I heard someone shout out, "Hey, gal!"

I thought, *That can't be Roc*. Immediately, I was pissed. He was in town and didn't warn me! I had to run into him.

Mr. Roc is a ladies' man. I'm his best friend and—when he is in town—the one his girlfriends call, all desperate to track him down.

As he got closer, Roc started off saying, "Shut your damn mouth. I do not want to hear it. I know I am wrong, but you know how I flow. I'm leaving on Sunday. I'll call you later."

When I went for the ice, this lady that looked like Mike Tyson in drag gave me this *Move out of the way, bitch* look. I ignored her; I wanted to leave the park with both of my ears.

I finally made it to the ice booth and, after getting the ice, I turned my phone off and started my trek to my seat. Forget trying to be cute, I was struggling to carry this five-pound bag of ice, the lemonade, and my purse. Not to mention, my "ta-tas" were trying their best to stay covered.

When I finally made it, my girls greeted me with sista love.

It is so good to treat yourself to real girlfriends. I mean, the kind that allow you to be you—provide unconditional love, no hating, not wanting your life or man, not trying to hustle you, are there rain or shine, stay out of your business, keep you on track, respect when you are in a relationship, and take care of you when you have had too much to drink.

Gypsy asked me to put the ice in the red cooler next to my seat. When I opened the top of the cooler, it was full of ice. Quickly looking at Gypsy, I asked, "Why in the hell do you need more ice?"

Laughing, she replied, "We don't. I was just messing with you."

I replied, "Not cute."

The youngest lady in the group, Michael (yes, a girl named Michael), had her catering company prepare all the food. Innocent, classy, and standing only four feet eleven, her hair was always in a neat ponytail with the cutest hair pins, and she spoke proper with that slow Southern drawl that lets you know she is from the old uptown Atlanta clan. Whenever Gypsy and I start talking trash, she responds with, "Now, ladies, we must remember to use our outside language while in the public."

I piled my plate with everything on the table. Before eating, I said, "Ladies, I have some bomb smoke. Let's fire up after I finish."

Gypsy replied, "I have some, too. Let's wait until dark."

Michael added, "No need to wait. The bag next to your chairs has my special cookies."

Holding my plate in one hand, I looked in the bag and asked, "Did you make these?"

"Yep," she said. "One of my clients gave me some smoke for a batch of my cookies, and I made extra for us." Suddenly, Michael got up to take a call. When she came back, she said, "That was Sylvie and Cindy."

Looking at Michael like she was crazy, I said, "Tell me you did not invite those mud-flap eyelash-wearing fake asses."

Smiling, Michael said, "Yes, I did. Joy, I know you don't like them, but I asked them to stop by for a bite. Please be nice."

Sitting up, I replied, "Me? Be nice? I guess you forgot how Cindy tried to embarrass me in front of my date at your card party when she asked me how many times I've been married."

Gypsy chimed in, "Yep, how could we forget the crazy look on your face when she smirked and said, 'So, you have lied to God six times.'"

Michael followed up with, "What got me was when you asked her if she was ashamed of staying in an unhappy marriage for thirty years and sleeping in separate bedrooms."

Sitting my drink on top of the red cooler, I said, "Damn real. I took her bully ass there. I loved that what-the-total-fuck-did-I-just-step-in look when I topped it off by asking if she'd host a baby shower for her husband's baby mama."

Michael sighed. "I guess it's true. You know what they say—the truth told with ill intent is worse than any lie you could ever invent."

Looking at Michael and Gypsy, I said, "Scared people will stay in a jacked-up situation because it is safe. They will bring everyone and everything around them down to make themselves feel better. As for me, baby, I ain't never scared of leaving any ass or anything. Why should I? God wants us to be happy. If you are not happy, then you might want to have a little talk with Jesus. To be honest, I am not happy. I am *joy-filled*. You can go to happy hour and leave sad, but joy never loses its energy. You become joy-filled, joyful, but have you ever heard of someone being happy-ful?"

Instead of answering, Michael rolled her eyes and replied, "Joy, you can and will make up some crazy shit."

Shaking her head, Gypsy asked, "Will you marry again?"

"Will I marry again?" I asked. "Damn real, until I get it right. Why stop trying? I think marriage is a noble institution, and I am looking to commit. Guess you really must be crazy to volunteer to be institutionalized. But I know no matter how dirty I get in life, God and my family love me unconditionally, even though I know family will have their jokes. Guess what? I am good with that. If you have God, best friends, and family, nothing else matters."

Feeling like I was talking to Karen, I changed the subject. "Ladies, guess who I ran into looking like 'Damn, I am busted'?"

Michael asked, "Lord, who?"

I started laughing and shouted, "Roc!"

Grabbing my leg, Gypsy responded, "You mean playboy Roc?"

Falling back in her chair, Michael said, "I know that he's your boy, but I tell you, the girls love his dirty socks. I cannot for the life of me figure out why."

"Yep, he has been my brother since the early nineties. I admit, he has his fan club, but that is not my business. If they put up with his shit, that's on them. But check this out—while we were at the beach, I went to his room to get the iron. When I knocked, he didn't answer, so assuming he was asleep, I tipped in. Baby girl, he was on his back on one side of the bed and his dick was hanging off the other side! When I saw that, I said to myself, 'Mystery solved.' If I had my phone, I would have taken a picture."

Both fell back as if they got hit by lightning.

"Oh, snap, ladies. Guess who else I ran into. Gus!" Gypsy gasped. "Heavy Gus?"

"We can't call him that now. This new Gus is fine as hell! He lost a ton of weight. Girls, he gave me a hug and a deep-throat kiss. I walked away with wet panties. Ladies, please help me remember why I took him out of my rotation."

Gypsy replied, "An ex will remind you why you stopped dealing with them."

"You are so right. We have dinner plans next week. I will keep you all posted," I replied. "Side note, on my way here, I noticed some of the ladies' hair. Now, I don't know for sure, but we might be the only women out showing our real hair."

Michael, looking puzzled, asked, "How in the hell do you know that?"

Taking a sip from my cup, I replied, "Well, hell, I didn't look at everyone's head for tracks, but you can tell when the hair doesn't match the person or when they have silky flowing hair and the kids' hair looks like a field of black pearls."

Gypsy said, "Joy, now that's a stretch. Maybe the kids took after the daddy."

With a raised eyebrow, I replied, "Hell, I don't know. Anyway, it breaks my heart to see so many lovely ladies hiding under the man's mad illusion of beauty. Like the vagina, your scalp is not made to be covered up. It needs air. It loves stroking. It requires trimming. It's happy when it is massaged. And most definitely, it needs to get wet. Just like dirt and impurities can give you bacteria or yeast infection, I am sure the combination of dried sweat, heat, dirt, dandruff, and hair products will have the same impact on your scalp. Let Roc tell it, dirty weave heads smell like chicken feet."

With an expression of disgust, Gypsy screamed, "That is why y'all are buddies! Both of you say some crazy shit. Lord, 'chicken feet?'"

"Work with me, ladies. Let me ask this, would you take someone else's pubic hair and glue it to your vagina? No? So, why do you take hair from who-knows-where and place it on your crown?"

Gypsy answered, "Makes sense, but vagina and freaking chicken feet? I'm done."

Instead of answering, Michael picked up my cup and smelled it, then asked, "What the hell are you drinking?"

Ignoring her, I said, "Okay, let me get off my soapbox. Enough of this low-vibing conversation. Let's walk over by the speakers and fire up. I am full and ready to party!"

On our way to the speakers, the DJ played our favorite Parliament song, "Atomic Dog." Like a moth to a flame, we rushed over to a group of Omegas to watch them step.

After they finished, we danced like we were getting paid until the end of the song.

Hot and high, we headed back to our seats. When we returned, sweating Michael said, "Damn, I needed that workout. Now I am ready to really party!"

Being me, to get a rise out of Michael, I said, "Sweetie, now that you are worked up, I guess Skutch—sorry I mean Darren—will be in for a treat."

Michael looked like I must have struck a nerve. "Joy, I wish you wouldn't call him that." She reached over and placed her small hands around my neck and whispered, "Say you're sorry."

Between my laughter, all I could say was, "Sorry, sorry, but you know he is a 'skutch'—a mofo that's beyond annoying, a low-vibing ass that loves to rattle your chain purposefully to piss you off."

With a napkin over her mouth, Gypsy said, "Can the church say amen?"

Micheal scrunched her face in frustration and said, "Gypsy, stop signifying Joy's foolishness."

When the last act took the stage, Michael suggested we start moving toward the exit. While we were gathering our things, she told us not to worry about the food table; her catering team would clean it up.

Gypsy stood up, stretching with her glass in one hand, and agreed with Michael. "Let's get a start on the crowd. I do *not* feel like walking behind a bunch of drunk, dehydrated, sleepy Black folks."

When we made it to the gate, Gypsy reached her long arms out and said, "Okay, girls. Group hug. Call me when you are in your locked cars."

CHAPTER 4

THE HELL WITH THIS

Michael

I enjoyed the concert, the laughs, the love, the fun. But now I was back to my misery.

I am so sad inside. Why did the universe put Darren into my life, a thirty-year-old alcoholic, abusive, heartless husband? The thought of my marriage made me cry. I was so tired—tired of fighting, tired of covering up, and tired of being tired. God, guide me through this madness, and let me be a better person on the backend.

Girl, pull it together. Enough of this low-level thinking.

It was good to see Mr. John, head of our estate's security, working the gate tonight. He stepped out of the guardhouse to greet me, flashing his warm smile. "Well, hello, Mrs. Sunshine."

"Hi, Mr. John. I see you are working late. How have you been?"

"All is good, love. How are you doing?"

"I'm good, just staying busy." Before pulling off, I asked, "Has my husband come through?"

He stopped smiling when he replied, "No, Sunshine, he hasn't."

I love coming in when Darren isn't home; his is energy is always so toxic. It's amazing how he can change my home into a house just by parking in the garage.

Damn, look how Darren left the kitchen. Shit is everywhere: jelly on the counter, the sink full of dirty dishes, and sausage grease splattered on the stove. Lord, he is one nasty ass. He made the mess; he could clean it up.

Hold the hell up. Tell me he did not *put an open jar of mayonnaise in the cabinet. I better put it in the trash before he kills someone. Second thought, he* is *the only person that eats this nasty shit. Forget tossing it. I give less than a damn if he gets food poisoning.*

I am going to bed. The hell with this.

Darren woke me when he came in and I pulled the covers over my head, pretending to be asleep. Peaking from under the covers, I saw him come into the room and stand over me. I felt like a lamb waiting to be slaughtered.

To take him out of his thoughts, I turned over. He tapped me on the shoulder and whispered in my ear, "Baby, are you asleep?"

I wanted to scream, *Get your stank breath out of my ear!* Pulling the covers back, I sat up and said, "Not now. What's up?"

He asked me about the concert and my girls, like he really gave a flip. I lied and said the girls thanked him so much for everything, especially the shrimp. Rubbing his head and looking around the room, he turned back and said, "I am glad someone can enjoy them. Since I had that reaction to the conch in the Bahamas, I've been careful about eating shellfish, you know?"

Thank God he was looking down because my face truly

showed how much I wished we would've run out of gas before reaching the hospital.

After the small talk, Darren finally got to what was really on his mind. "Baby—look, I have to pick my clients up from the airport in the morning, and I really need to use your SUV."

"Sure." I faked a yawn and told him to take my briefcase out of the trunk and put it in my office. I said goodnight and rolled over.

CHAPTER 5

DO RIGHT OR TOSS SALAD

Darren

I better clean out the car before I hand it over to Michael, even though I really don't have to worry. She knows what I would do to her if I caught her going through my shit.

My godmother, Jackie Mae, was spot on when she advised me to marry Michael. She's manageable, almost like being with a white girl—so fucking gullible. Heaven knows, she kills me with that I-just-love-my-man look. If she only knew my journey to marrying her boring ass.

Growing up, I loved spending time with my godparents, Clifford and Jackie Mae. If I had to guess, I think Jackie Mae was thirty. Clifford had been her twelfth-grade teacher, and two years after her graduation they were married. My understanding, Jackie Mae used to be a "lady of the night." In other words, she sold pussy.

Jackie Mae was different from the other ladies in my parents' circle, but she perfectly fit anyway. She was bold when it came to living her life, but they all had the same survival skills when it came to manipulating men. Looking back, I think they all had a little Jackie Mae in them.

Clifford loved Jackie Mae, and he knew how she rolled. When he traveled, he would ask me to stay with her to "keep her company." He said she was "scared" to be in their big house all alone. I think *he* was just scared to leave her to herself.

At one of my parents' parties just before my seventeenth birthday, Jackie Mae pulled me aside and said, "I know your birthday is next week, but can you stay with me tomorrow? Clifford has to go out of town for a couple of days."

I thought, *She is a grown-ass woman. What kind of protection am I going to provide? If someone does break in, I'm going to hide under them big tits of hers.* Laughing to myself, I told her, "Sure, no problem. I'd love to hang out with you."

Smiling, Jackie Mae said, "Great. I'll pick you up tomorrow around noon."

The next day, Jackie Mae called to let me know she was on her way to pick me up. After packing a bag, I went outside to wait for her. As soon as I closed the house door, she pulled up in a brand-new white sports car. "Hey, baby boy."

Walking around the car, I said, "Damn, Jackie Mae, when did you get this?"

While letting the top down, Jackie Mae told me, "Clifford ordered it last month. Just picked it up today. Get in." Then, before pulling off, Jackie Mae said, "Baby, I know it is your birthday, so I tell you what. Let's do dinner, your choice."

With my head laying back on the white headrest, I suggested picking up some movies and pizza.

Reaching back behind my seat to get her lipstick, she

said, "Let's do it." She put on her scarf, freshened her already-red lips, and hit the gas.

When we got around the corner, she made a right turn on Main Street, and we drove for about ten minutes in complete silence. Without warning, she pulled the car over, reached forward, and turned the radio up. "Do you want to drive, birthday boy?"

Acting like the sixteen-year-old I was, I said, "Jackie Mae, are you kidding?"

Before she could answer, she was already climbing out of the car. Keep in mind, my parents were drunks. So, I had to drive their passed-out asses home all the time. When I made it home, I would get out of the car and leave them in there. To this day, they still don't remember who drove them home all those times.

While reaching for the driver's door, I looked over at Jackie Mae. She was sitting there, lips ruby red, legs crossed, and her right arm resting on the door. For a moment, I felt like she was my woman and I was her man. As we sped down the freeway, Jackie threw her hands in the air and screamed like she was coming down the world's tallest roller coaster.

When we got to her house, I parked the car next to the large fountain in the center of the circular drive. Jackie Mae got out of the car and took my bag in while I raised the top.

Walking into Clifford and Jackie Mae's house was like walking into a fancy beach house. The large window in the living room gave a perfect view to the pool and hot tub.

As I locked the door, I heard Jackie Mae call, "Come in here, baby boy."

Knowing her, I knew she would be somewhere near the bar. Soon as I walked into the room, she was standing with her back facing me. When she turned around, I saw this lovely birthday cake with one happy-face candle.

"Wow, Jackie Mae, thank you." I sat down while she sang me a sweet version of "Happy Birthday." I blew out the candle, then we both sat and enjoyed a slice of heaven.

"Jackie Mae, thanks again for letting me drive your new car."

"You are welcome, baby. Enjoy your cake." Handing me the remote, she said, "Make yourself at home." Then she just disappeared.

Damn, my birthday is kicking off like a young player. I cannot believe she just handed me the keys to her brand-new car.

Leaning back on the sofa, I turned on the TV, but before I was able to find something good, I felt myself nodding off. The smell of Jackie Mae's perfume woke me up. When I opened my eyes, she was standing right over me. Rubbing my forehead, she said, "Baby, go take your shower. We can have the pizza delivered."

I staggered into the bathroom, turned on the shower, and stood in front of the mirror admiring the hint of facial hair growing around my mouth until steam engulfed the room.

When I stepped in, I adjusted the massaging showerhead, held my head back, and closed my eyes. Out of the blue, I felt a breeze from the bathroom blend with the shower's steam. When I opened my eyes, Jackie Mae had the curtain in one hand as she stepped her naked body into the shower with me. My shocked eyes locked on her tits, looking like two new soccer balls. I wasn't sure if the water was making me grow or if it was making Jackie Mae shrink, because slowly, I could see the top of her head as she kneeled before me. By this time, she was eye to eye with my dick, then her mouth came closer, and I felt *it* sitting on her tongue.

With her mouth around me, my mind went straight

from porn movies to the actual sensation I was introduced to. The sight of her moving back and forth, feeling my dick rubbing on the side of her mouth and hitting the back of her throat, made my legs start to vibrate. While I rubbed her soft, wet hair, my eyes rolled back.

Suddenly, thinking I had to pee, I tried to pull back, but she was holding my butt so tight all I could do was nothing. After my soft dick slid out of her mouth, she looked up at me and said, "Baby, this is your lucky day."

From that day on, she would show her "love" for me anytime and anywhere she could.

A week after my birthday surprise, I was arrested for receiving stolen property, driving with a suspended license, and resisting arrest. *Shit and damn, I am in big trouble. Lord, help me get out of my situation. You know I wouldn't make it one day in prison.*

My lawyer said it did not look good. In the past, he could get my case thrown out, but not this time. My fate would be in the hands of a jury.

My father had been hell to deal with since my latest charges. Staying at home was one of the conditions of my bond, but by the way he'd been acting, I should have just stayed in jail until my trial. This house was enormous enough for me to do me, but he was closing in the walls. The basement went from my fun place to shelter from my parents. My only friends were eating and drinking. I bet I gained ten pounds while in house arrest.

The smell of breakfast woke me up. When I got to the kitchen, Ms. Wonda, our housekeeper since I was five years old, was standing at the stove making breakfast. "Hi, baby. How are you feeling?"

Trying not to look too sad, I walked over and gave her a big hug. "I'm fine, just a little stressed."

Kissing the side of my face, she patted my back. At that moment I felt like all would be good. "Baby, sit down while I fix your plate."

When she placed my plate in front of me, my pancakes had eyes, a nose, and a smile, and my favorite cheesy omelet sat on top like a yellow head of hair. For a moment, I was able to glimpse her concern, and the sadness in her voice broke my heart. We usually sat and talked over breakfast, but today she treated me like my parents, showing no love.

After I finished eating, I told her how much I appreciated her and headed back to the basement. The only thing on my mind was running the streets that were suddenly calling my name, sharing a strategy on how I could escape. I found myself standing at the front door.

Just as I reached for the knob, my father stepped around the corner. Without breaking his stride, he got right in my face. "Boy, I dare you to touch that doorknob."

Saying nothing, I just turned, and—like a little boy—I walked straight to the basement like I was going to time out.

The night before my trial, I woke up to Ms. Wonda standing over me with her head down, holding her Bible tight to her heart. As she stood in complete silence, I could feel her tears fall on my hand. I could hear a soft whimper as she reached for the cross around her neck. Then I heard, "Amen."

The morning of my trial, my parents did not say a word to me: no "Good morning," no "Baby, be strong," no "I love you," nothing.

When we got to the courthouse, I noticed my attorneys and a bruiser-looking man in a blue suit standing on the curb. After my father pulled to the curb, the man in the blue suit opened the driver's door and my father stepped out. "Mr. Blue Suit" took over the wheel as my father walked around to open my mother's door, and they stood next to the car and chatted with one of the attorneys. Without looking back, my parents walked away.

The guy behind the wheel said, "Get out."

I replied, "That's it? Just 'Get out'? No 'Good luck,' no moment of prayer, just 'Get out'?"

I sat there for a second, looking in the rear-view mirror. He locked his eyes with mine in the mirror and shouted, "Get the hell out."

Slowly, I opened the door and got out, not saying a word. The attorney standing at the curb escorted me to the courtroom.

Before the trial started, I saw my attorneys standing at the prosecutor's table. My eyes moved from them to the empty jury box. Suddenly I heard, "All rise."

To my shock, I knew the judge. She was one of the drunks from my parents' parties.

When my case came up, it became clear why the jury box was empty. With shocked eyes and listening ears, I heard my attorney tell the judge their client had agreed to plead nolo contendere, and an agreement had been worked out with the prosecutors.

As I stood up for my sentence, the judge looked at me like I was a man given his last chance. "Mr. Humphrey, I see you are seventeen years old with no criminal record."

I thought, *Thanks to my parents' connections*. "Yes, Your Honor."

"Son, I am going to give you a chance to turn your life around. You have three options, one of which you'll have to decide on today. One: become a soldier. Two: become a college student. Or three: become a prisoner. So, sign up for a form of armed services, go to college, or go to jail. Which option will you take?"

Thinking, *I don't like anyone telling me what to do, so being a solider is not an option, and I do not like tossing salad, so jail isn't an option. I guess it is going to be option number two,* I leaned over to my attorney and said I would like to go to college. The terms of my deal: I had one year on probation, thirty days community service, and not only had to go to college—but to graduate.

After talking to my attorney, I turned to see my parents' reaction only to find the only person behind me was Ms. Wonda, looking at me as she wiped her eyes.

I found my parents outside on the curb. When I walked up, I knew better than to utter a word. Mr. Blue Suit pulled up in our car, stepped out, and we all got in. As we pulled off, for some strange reason I could not take my eyes off the front of the courthouse. At that moment, I decided not only was I going to college, but I would go to law school, and one day I would stand in front of the bench I just walked away from.

When I got home all I could do was take a nap. Like the night before, half asleep, I saw Ms. Wonda standing over me, holding her Bible. After she said, "Amen," I could hear her crying. On her way out of the room, I heard her say, "Lord, help this child. It's not his fault he ain't shit."

All my family went to college at FAMU in Tallahassee. I decided if it was good enough for them, it was good enough for me. I tried to call my Grandma Rosie—my father's mom, who was now living in Jamaica—to share my plan to go to college, but never could reach her. As I thought about it, we were never close. She was always there to hand out money, but it was more out of obligation than love.

The day before I left for Tallahassee, Tee, my mother's mother, and I had lunch at her favorite restaurant, Hattie's

Food for the Soul. Now, what really gets me about my family is how they try too hard not to be Black, but they can eat the hell out a plate of some soul food.

Over lunch, Tee shared how proud she was and told me she had my back. Then she said, "Baby, when you get on campus, find a wife that 'looks like us.'"

Ever since I was a kid, she drove home how we had to keep the look in the family. Having a baby by the wrong woman could change the flavor of the ice cream.

"Make sure that she loves you so much, she will allow you to *be* you."

Being in this family, I knew what that meant: high yellow, gullible, and manageable.

With a stern look, Tee said, "Son, yes, I am proud of you, but I don't feel like you are ready to manage your trust, so I changed the trust agreement. The revised terms are you must be married and have at least one child before the trust is transferred over to you. Do you understand what is expected of you?" But before I could answer, she asked, "So, Darren, baby, have you heard from your Grandma Rosie?"

I thought, *Why is she asking about Rosie, and what the fuck is up with my trust?* I said, "No, she is in Jamaica. Why do you ask?"

Looking like she does when she's trying to manipulate my mom, she said, "Well, I know she has the funds to help you out, so do not lose connection with her."

"I tried to reach her, but last time we connected, she seemed somewhat distant. Funny—sometimes, instead of calling me back, she just deposits a couple of dollars in my account. You know, Tee, sometimes she makes me feel like I am a burden she has to tolerate." *To be honest, my dad makes me feel the same way. I never felt like he was proud I was his son.* Looking at Tee, I asked, "Do you know why they treat me like I'm not wanted?"

Instead of answering my question, Tee ordered another drink. When our food arrived, Tee said, "Boy, stop. They treat all of your mom's side of the family that way. Stop thinking like that. I am sure your dad is proud to be your father and you are not a burden to anyone in our family."

I heard what Tee was saying, but I knew what my heart was telling me: I was a burden to both my father and Rosie. They didn't love me. I was just being tolerated.

My parents insisted I live on campus my first year. That meant sharing a room with a stranger, going down the hall to shit and shower, going to the campus dining room, and living amongst people that I couldn't control.

Yet.

For the first time in my life, I was on my own—not just on my own, but without my parents' protection. Living on campus had its advantages. For once, I had time to get up on the young girls and make notes of who was fucking and sucking. The assortment of free pussy amazed me—not to lay up in, but to cash in on.

But I needed to stay focused. Jackie Mae used to tell me, "Them girls out there who slang pussy make it hard for a true hoe. Keep the dick in your pants and keep your money separate."

But the judge told me to go to college. She never mentioned how I had to conduct myself once I got there. It took me a minute to totally detox—physically and mentally. Thank the Lord the judge didn't require a drug test. If so, I'd be tossing salad.

One day, I was sitting in front of the dorm wondering what I needed to stay in the game, when I saw this pretty young thang come up the stairs walking like she never had a real dick: bright-eyed, innocent, and ready for grooming. I asked her name, and she said, "Michael."

Soon as she spoke, I quickly surmised that she would be putty in these devilish hands of mine. To top it off, her simple beauty met my parents' daughter-in-law criteria: long hair, soft features, and skin that was lighter than a paper bag.

We sat and talked. She shared that she had her own apartment and a car. As far as I was concerned, I was in love. So, I hid my past, and I started to play the role of a square. Before the semester ended, I pretty much moved into her place.

In that first year, I focused on studying, staying out of trouble, and keeping Michael happy. Truth be told, if Tee didn't approve of her, I would dump her boring ass. Now, if she *did* approve, I planned on marrying her, getting her pregnant, and getting my fucking inheritance.

In the start of my second year, my parents bought me a new car, and I guess Tee was tired of hearing me complain about staying in the dorms because she bought me a small house near campus.

Tee and Jackie Mae came up for a week to help me set my new place up. Tee stayed with her good friend Ms. Judy, which was fine with me because it gave me some "alone time" with Jackie Mae.

During dinner, Jackie Mae mentioned my trust. With a serious look, Jackie Mae asked, "From what Tee shared, your inheritance hinges on marriage and a baby. I am sure you are aware of the terms, correct?"

With a flippant response, I said, "That's what she told me. I never saw the agreement."

Shocked at my attitude, Jackie Mae replied, "Baby, Tee did make the changes. She showed me the agreement. I know she is going to support you until you finish school and get a job. After that, you're on your own. I encourage you to stay focused."

Placing my fork down, I told Jackie Mae, "I know what I need to do. Matter of fact, I'm working on it as we speak. Last year, I met a girl that meets my family's main criteria: she 'looks like us.' Her name is Michael. I'm sure Tee and my parents will love her."

With a concerned look, Jackie Mae replied, "So, baby boy, I see you have your family's love covered, but do *you* love her?"

"As of now, I like her, and I love what she brings to the table—the path to my inheritance. To be honest, I need to leave college with a future wife. I am not wasting my time courting her after college. My plan is to marry her, dump her in a big house, get her pregnant, and get back to doing whatever I want."

"Sounds like Michael is in your cross hair. Like it or love it, she has to be your main girl. Make sure you keep her confident and never—I mean *never*—let your outside girls make their presence known to her. Another thing, Darren, don't make her hard or bitter. Stay out the corner of her eye, and play hide-the-dick. Never dick her down; you can dick down the women you don't care about. Just keep giving her the square dick. Don't turn your future wife on to the freak game, and *don't* you get hooked on her pussy. If you do, then you will be her boy-bitch."

With a chuckle, I replied, "Jackie, speaking of laying the square dick, the other night Michael came over in nothing but this black lace teddy and a raincoat. I wanted so badly to dick her down, but instead I screwed her like I had one arm and one leg.

"After we finished, she ran to the bathroom. Looking

through the half-closed door, I could see her wiping that sorry pussy off with my brand-new towels. When she came out, I was still laying on the bed with my dick flopped to the side, rubber hanging on like a nightcap. Suddenly, I felt her lift my dick and wipe it off. She didn't dare touch the rubber, but in one quick swoop, she wiped my dick, and when she turned around, I looked down at my dick without the hanging cap. I raised my head to see how she was going to dispose of the rubber and almost hollered when I saw her standing over the toilet, shaking the towel like she was handwashing dirty draws.

"When she came back and sat next to me, she said, 'Baby, you must've enjoyed that, the way you are smiling.' I told her, 'Baby, every time we make love, I think about how lucky I am.'"

The last night of Tee and Jackie Mae's visit, I invited Michael over for dinner. When she walked in, I saw the happiness all over Tee's face. Reaching out to hug Michael, she said, "Baby, you look like *my* people."

Jackie Mae was happy to know she did not have bedroom competition.

And I was elated thinking about how close I was to my money.

CHAPTER 6

DOG PIMPING

Joy

It was eleven p.m., and I had been listening to sleep music for over an hour. Instead of falling asleep, my mind was everywhere, from how I overate at dinner to wondering if I locked the car door.

Oh, well. No need to be up alone. Let's give Ms. Gypsy a call.

Answering on the first ring, she said, "Hey, girl, why in the hell are you calling me at eleven?"

"Why in the hell are you answering your phone on the first ring? To be honest, I called to tell you I can't sleep. So, why are you up this late?" I laughed.

In her matter-of-fact voice, she said, "What's new? You're always up. I was thumbing through my new Chef Carmen ATL cookbook I received yesterday. So, what is the dog pound up to?"

"Girl, I think Maxx is crazy. Check this out—last night these fools woke me up at one a.m. to go do what the hell they do. When we get outside, they started barking at three deer in my backyard. Now I am standing in the shadows, butt-naked, whispering, 'Be the hell quiet.' As expected, Maxx runs after the deer, so I grab the coat by the door and run after him, while TJ lookin' at us like, 'What the hell is going on?' Luckily, I was able to catch Maxx before he ran into the neighbor's yard. I wanted to choke him, but he's so cute, all I could do was hug him.

"When we got back inside, they started barking and running around until I gave them a treat. Now, I figured it's dark, so they couldn't see I broke the dog treat in half. I reached down to give it to them quickly and ran upstairs. Before I hit the second step, Maxx gets to barking like, 'Oh, hell nah! Us know *half* when we taste it.' Then TJ joins in and looks at Maxx like, 'I am feeling you, man.'"

Laughing until she started to cough, Gypsy said, "Girl, I told you they act just like you."

"You might be right. My mom sent me a box of mangos. Stop by tomorrow to pick up some."

After laughing at my madness, we both said our goodbyes.

Lying there, I thought, *Some girls think because I really don't give two cents about dropping a man or because I make it look easy living on my own that I don't think how it'd be nice to be somebody's baby, and not be a girl all on my own.*

(Now, don't get me wrong. I was not having Phyllis Hyman moment; I was not depressed. Trust me, I know. I have been checked.)

It would have been nice to roll over and whisper in some sweet thang's ear, "It's your turn to let them out."

Girl, you need to stop.

CHAPTER 7

I HATE TO AGREE

Joy

I woke up to two missed calls. Funny, I only heard the phone ring once. First call was from Gus and the second from Gypsy. Sista love first.

In my Valley Girl tone, I said, "Hello, may I speak to Ms. Gypsy?"

"May I ask who is calling?"

I screamed, "Hell, no, heifer!" We both fell out laughing.

She said, "Fool, what do you want?"

"I should be asking you that, sweetie. You called me."

"Sorry, I sure did. I know you carry that phone around like a pet rock, so what were you doing you couldn't answer the phone?"

"Nothing much—just finishing up a well-earned dump."

"Damn, Joy, TMI! TMI!"

Laughing at her reaction, I said, "So, gal, what's up?"

With an earnest tone, she said, "It's Michael. She wants us to meet her for brunch tomorrow. I confirmed for you. Hope that's okay. Joy, I need you to give Michael some slack about Darren. You know you really struck a nerve the other night at the park."

"I know. That was my intent. to be honest I was being nice. I'm letting her know I know the real deal."

"Real deal? Fool, what are you talking about? Hold up, now let me take the chance and ask you something. I assume you know 'the real deal?'" Gypsy sounded confused.

"Yes, I do, and so do you, Gypsy. You saw those handprints on her arm when we were at the beach."

"Yes, I did. She said she got it from playing around in the pool with Darren."

I wanted to scream. "Cool, that's what she calls it. I call it an ass beating."

"Joy, what in the hell are you talking about?"

"Look, I know the signs of getting beat by a man."

"Joy, just because some old, married fool kicked your butt does not make you an expert on domestic violence."

"True, but he *kicked my ass*. She is *getting beat*," I emphasized.

With a loud sigh, Gypsy said, "I'm afraid to ask, but is there a difference?"

"Yes, but I'm not going there, Gypsy. And another thing, I bet you money he is fooling around on her. Look, I'm out here in the streets. It is just a matter of time before I run up on him. I'll back off, but I still have my eye on her. She is such a sweetheart. I just hate to see her have to go through this."

"Joy, I understand your point, but she is grown. Remember, a tree cannot grow in the shade. Stand back and let her stand in the sun. She will be okay. She has us, but most of all she has a strong faith. God is watching out for her."

"All right, all right already. I'll back off, but let me catch his ass," I said. "Gypsy, I'm good with brunch. Let's ride together in case I get so pissed I have to drink to calm my nerves."

Lord, I cannot believe these girls. Gypsy is living in a dream world, and Michael is living a nightmare, but they are still my girls.

***

Gypsy

After talking to Joy, I admit this: she has been correct twice today. She was so correct when she said there was a difference between an "ass kicking" and someone "beating your ass." Based on my experience dealing with Joy and her Messes, when someone kicks your ass, it's usually a pleasant person who has been pushed to their limit and just snapped. When a person beats you, there is a science behind it. The inflictor's intent is to degrade, demean, demoralize, and control another person. If the victim is pushed to the limit, then the victim will survive by "beating their ass." Just ask Tina. Ike beat her, but in the end, she kicked his ass in that limo in Texas. Slaves were beat, but the masters got their ass kicked during the Civil War. Michael, innocent and trusting, reminds me so much of me at one time, which is why I'm sure Joy is correct. I noticed Michael the other day at the mall. She was shy about taking her clothes off in the open dressing room. I said nothing, but what really confirmed things was that she must get broken nails fixed every week, sometimes twice a week. The Michael I know is careful about her nails, even to the point where she is always asking us to open her drink can. Lord, help me control Joy and help me guide Michael to freedom.

CHAPTER 8

DON'T SAY A WORD

Joy

I really love this Bluetooth in my car. I connected it after I got stopped for "texting"—even though I really was just trying to find Gypsy in my contact list—but Ms. Lady Cop pulled me over and gave me a boring lecture about texting and driving. Then she had the nerve to say, "A car this nice should have Bluetooth," and of course I had a dumb look on my face.

Why? Because she was correct. I had been too lazy to connect it.

After the lecture, she was sweet enough to give me a warning. I thanked her and kept it moving.

"Siri, call Gypsy."

Instead of saying hello, Gypsy said, "Girl, I picked the phone up to call you!"

I learned long ago not to react to my foresight. I just said, "I am on my way."

"Why did you call?" she asked.

"I'm on your street. Oh, also, I wanted to know, uh, are you going to wear a hat?"

She replied, "For sure. Michael asked us to wear our beach hats to kick-off summer."

Driving up her driveway, I thought, *I should blow the horn, but she hates when someone does that. Oh, well, this is a good day to piss her off.*

I laid on the horn until she came to the door. She walked up to the car and just stood there for a couple of seconds looking me straight in the eye, then she said in a slow, calculated tone, "I will not respond to your madness. Let's go."

Before we got on I-285 North, Gypsy started telling me how to act. "Look, I know you mean well, but please do not start calling Darren 'Skutch,' and take it easy on Michael. Poor thing. Trust me, she does not need your foolishness today."

Knowing Gypsy, I thought she knew more than she was saying. "Gypsy, come clean. Is there something you're not telling me?"

With her face turned to her window, she said, "What makes you say that?" I did not open my mouth. She reached over and turned the music down. With a real stern look, she said, "I think you're right about Michael. I really think Darren is being physical with her."

My only response was, "Damn, Gypsy, tell me what the hell you know. Lord, I feel like I am picking damn cotton."

"My girl Trisha from the hair salon mentioned while she was washing Michael's hair that she noticed bruises around her neck. She said nothing. Coming out of an abusive marriage, she had a strong feeling something wasn't right."

By this time, I just lost it. "So, let me get this straight. You believe me *now*. Like my ass-kicking from the married man meant nothing."

"Damn, Joy, you need to stop with your crap. Please,

not today. I am serious. We need to do something—I just don't know what."

"How about turning the car around and shooting his bully ass?" I said matter-of-factly.

"Joy, stop playing. Look, we cannot repeat what Trisha shared."

Agreeing, I said, "I know. I've been thinking the same thing. Let's just watch her, and if I can bring up the conversation, I will." I could tell Gypsy was worried, and of course we were both hurt for our friend.

When we got to the mall, traffic was horrible and parking was limited. "Valet park. I'm hungry and need a drink," Gypsy grumbled. When we got out the car, Gypsy started in on me. "Promise me you don't start that Skutch shit. If you do—"

Without looking around I asked, "Gal, if I do, what?"

When we walked into the restaurant, I thought about Darren hitting Michael and whispered a prayer, "Dear God, please help me control my mouth and temper. I promised Gypsy I wouldn't say anything."

After waiting for a few minutes, the host checked our reservation and escorted us to our seats. As soon as we were seated, Michael walked in with this pretty, pink summer hat and a huge, matching silk scarf around her neck. We got up and gave Michael a big group hug. Before sitting, Michael said, "Order a bottle of wine." Then she excused herself and ran to the ladies' room.

With amazement, we both looked at each other, then Gypsy said, "Lord, I think Trisha is right. Do you see how she has that big scarf wrapped around her neck? Damn thing looks like a neck brace."

Watching Michael walk back to the table, I whispered to Gypsy, "Do you notice her eyes? They look so sad."

"Yes, I did notice. The sad look and that damn scarf concern me," Gyspy replied, covering her mouth.

When Michael returned, Gypsy and I did most of the talking.

Sounding excited, Gypsy said, "Guess what? I presented my business plan to the bank for my country retreat last week, and the bank approved the one-million-dollar loan application! Thanks to the both of you for pulling everything together. Michael, the bank loved your idea about having an on-site cafeteria instead of outsourcing the food preparation."

"Gypsy, I enjoyed working on your plan, and I am so proud of you! I figured they would like the idea of using local produce instead of catering. Why not? You're on a farm," Michael said.

"Let's make a toast to happy times and happy places." I picked up my glass. "Wait. We need to do a pajama party at the farm! You know Roc has a new Winnebago? I'm going to get him to drive us down."

"Do you think he would?" Michael asked.

"Damn real, he will. As much as I cover for him, he better. Otherwise, I'll tell his women all his business. Anyway, if he can't drive us down, I'm sure he'll let us use it. So, are we going to do it?"

"Hell yeah," Gypsy and Michael said together.

"Let me give him a call now."

Answering on my first ring, Roc said, "What? Make it fast. I'm in the middle of something."

"First of all, tell your women to stop calling me. When I get a moment, I'll forward all their messages—but that's not why I am calling, Michael wants to borrow your Winnebago for a ladies' outing next month."

I could hear the smile in his voice. "You mean cute Michael?"

Not responding, I followed up with, "And Gypsy wants to know if you would drive."

"Okay, now let me ask—what does Joy want?"

Pausing, I said, "I want you to say yes and yes."

Roc laughed. "Three against one is not fair, but I'm game." Then he told me he loved me and just hung up.

Placing the phone down, I said, "He said yes." *He better.*

Michael volunteered to pay for lunch and suggested we walk to the mall to pick up matching pajamas for our pajama party. Suddenly, Michael received a call that seemed to break her spirit. The more she talked, the more she looked like a scared little girl.

I stood close to her so I could hear what was going on. I could hear Darren screaming at her, "Your dumb ass brought my car back with the gas light on, and now I have to stop for gas! This is going to make me late for my appointment!"

When he said that, tears just slowly rolled down her face.

Then he told her, "I bet you're out with your skank girlfriends. You are going to be nothing, just like them. Bring your broke-down ass home *now!*"

When he said that, she just dropped her head and hung up.

Did this mofo just call us skanks and say she was broke down? I thought. Of course, I couldn't say anything, but I felt both of my fists getting tight. In my mind, I could see myself holding him down while she kicked him in the nuts.

After she hung up, both Gypsy and I asked what was wrong, but Michael said, "No worries, it was Darren being Darren."

Before I could give my opinion, Gypsy said, "Let's do a group hug." So, we put Michael in the middle and just loved on her right in the middle of the mall. She was so sad, I could feel her little body tremble.

When we left the mall, I shared with Gypsy what I heard and how I was glad she intervened. "I wanted to snatch that phone from Michael and give his disrespectful ass a piece of my mind!"

"Joy, trust me—I saw," said Gypsy. "You had the crazy look in your eyes. That's why I asked for the group hug."

We both sat in the car in complete silence. When I looked over at Gypsy, I saw tears in her eyes. Seeing her face and thinking about Michael made my heart ache.

Right in the middle of my favorite song, Gypsy had the nerve to turn my damn music down again. She started looking through that suitcase of a purse and, without looking up, she said, "You know, you really need to go see someone about your hyper personality. I am telling you, it is not normal for you to be *so* off the chain twenty hours a day, and your crazy butt don't sleep but four hours a day." Then she got louder: "I am telling you, honey, that is not normal!"

Here I was, trying to enjoy my music, riding in the fast lane with the top down, thinking about the trouble our baby girl was going through, and Gypsy had the nerve to complain about *me*. As she continued assessing my personality, I gradually moved from the fast lane to the emergency lane. Before she knew it, we were sitting on the side of I-285, big hats on.

Let her finish her one-way conversation.

I turned the car off and turned to face her, and with a very straight face said, "Gypsy, I didn't want to tell you this, but since you opened the door, I might as well take a seat. Do you remember the night I spent at your place, and we fell asleep watching our favorite movie, *J. D.'s Revenge*?"

She looked at me with this *What-the-hell* look, and sarcastically said, "Yes, and what?"

"Well, I did not want to say this, but in your sleep, you

started crying and in a little-girl voice said, 'You did us wrong, you did me wrong, and now you have the nerve to die.' If anyone needs help, your Gemini self should make the first appointment."

Gypsy looked at me with a blank look before she just started bawling her eyes out. Now, this is Ms. Jo Cool. Nothing rattles her, yet she just lost it. After she got herself together, she told me how she has been crying for no apparent reason and how she couldn't sleep. Suddenly, we both fell into each other's arms right on I-285 South and just sobbed.

Suddenly, we saw blue lights behind us, and here came Ms. Lady Cop walking slowly up to the back of the car again. I am sure having the top down didn't help. The officer asked if everything was okay, and we assured her we were not crazy.

She told us, "Please keep it moving. As you can tell, you are impacting rush-hour traffic."

We both slowly looked around. To our surprise, I-285 South traffic was backed up as far as the eye could see with all the rubbernecks.

When I pulled off, we both made a promise to schedule time as soon as possible with a therapist. I think we both needed to exhale before we had to post bail.

We sat quietly, listening to the jazz station until I pulled into Gypsy's driveway. Reaching to turn the music down, Gypsy said, "I think the pajama party will be a good time to talk to Michael."

"I'll get Michael some smoke and get her high. She'll talk. Better than that, I'll add some alcohol, then I will get her naked and dust her for handprints."

After I said that, we both looked at each other and laughed, feeling our mood lighten. Afterward, Gypsy gave me a big hug and we parted ways.

CHAPTER 9

FREE YOUR MONKEY MIND

Joy

After my conference call, I called Michael.

"Michael, this is Joy. I wanted to thank you for lunch. You know, Gypsy and I love you like a baby sister and we are both concerned about you. Something seems amiss lately."

"I'm not doing well—I'm sure you could tell from my reaction to Darren's phone call when we were at the mall. I am so sorry for making you all worry and for not opening up, but it is so hard for me to admit to anyone how unhappy I am," Michael said.

"Baby, you don't have to explain. However, let me share something with you from my past. I know the signs of abuse—physical and mental. You have all the signs: bruises, constant broken nails, and the expressions on your face tell it all. Let me ask you this question. Why are you staying with Darren? I know it is not financial. From what you shared, Darren's grandmother—his dad's mother, Rosie—made sure you're taken care of, right?"

Michael said, "Correct. Rosie did leave me half of her estate. Why me instead of her only grandchild? I ask myself the same question over and over. I'm not sure if I'm staying out of fear of the dating game. Darren was my first boyfriend. Just my luck, I would end up with another Darren or someone worse than Darren, if that was possible. I hope Darren will change his evil ways and we could put the worst behind us."

She paused a minute, then said, "Watching my parents—no matter what issue they had to face, they stayed together. Their view was, when you make a promise to God, you stick to it, for better or worse. I asked my parents how they stayed together for over forty years. They said, 'Find your happy place in the mist of your unhappy place.' My catering business and my bond with you and Gypsy make me happy."

"Michael, that is your parents' creed, but this is *your* life. Relationship issues and abuse should not be compared. Relationship issues are situations that two people can work out, but abuse of any kind is not a relationship issue. It is a control and mental issue, something that is toxic and could be deadly."

"Joy, I get that, but not everyone is as strong as you are."

"Baby, what do you mean?"

"Joy, I watch how you move in and out of relationships without a second thought. That takes strength—strength that I do not have right now."

With confidence, I replied, "Yes, it takes strength to move on and not go back, but it is 'the knowing' that pushes you through—knowing that God has taken care of me and will always take care of me. I look at it like this.

My ex-messes were men I picked, not what God chose for me. The man he has for me will be right for me. God gives us free will. When I make a bad choice, I don't sit in it. I move on. That's why I'm not giving up on marriage. I will marry the right man, and I am hoping he will be Husband Number Seven and not Mess Number Seven. Michael, baby, I truly love you. I want you to fight for what is your right, by any means necessary."

Sounding puzzled, Michael, asked, "What do you mean 'your right?'"

"I mean, what is right for Queen Michael—not for your parents, not for your spouse, and not for church folk. I'll share a funny story about how my daddy made my sweet sister, Lily, fight. Lily is three years older than me. Growing up, I was taller and more playground-tough while she was sweet, gentle, and had long, black, silky curls that rested on her thin shoulders. To be honest, baby girl, you remind me of her.

"How so?"

I smiled, "Well, like Lily you aren't a brawler, which isn't a bad thing, at times. But you have a "Joy" in your life who will support you and sometimes brawl *for* you. If you have time, I'd love to tell you a funny story from our childhood."

"Sure!" Michael said. "I love you childhood stories. Your delivery makes me feel like I'm actually there!"

"Awe, thanks, baby girl. I can remember like it was yesterday. I was sitting on our back porch when Lily came running home—dress dirty, wearing only one shoe, and her big toe sticking through the hole in her sock. Daddy was in the kitchen cooking. Like a lion hearing his cub in distress, he ran outside, looking in my sister's direction. With a white dish towel still hanging over his shoulder, he stood at the top of the stairs when Lily jumped straight into his arms. He held her, and in a slow Southern drawl whispered, 'Baby, what is wrong with you?'

"I could hear her telling him the big girl next door, Pudding, called her a half-breed and beat her up. Now, I sat there thinking, *Heck no*. I jumped off the porch and looked straight toward Pudding's house.

"Once Daddy understood Lily was not running from some wild beast, he slowly tried to put her down, but she just held on like a spider monkey. When he finally pried her claws off, he stood her right in front of him, pointed toward the brick pile in the backyard, and said, 'Turn your scared little tail around and bring me a brick.' She stood for a second, confused.

"I knew what was up—this wasn't the first time he made her fight. Still, I could not believe it. He was preparing her for battle—this time with a brick!

"Head hanging, crying, Lily slowly walked off and came back with a little broken brick. Before she even made it to the porch, Daddy raised his arm and pointed at her, saying, 'I said a brick, not a rock.'

"I walked with her back to the pile of bricks. Lord, I was trying to handle so many emotions. I was mad as hell. I wanted to cry with her, but I had to be strong. If I cried, knowing her, she would just cry harder.

"When we were out of Daddy's view, I reached down and grabbed a brick—not any brick, but a brick with cement on both sides. I pulled her hand out and put it right into her palm. I told her, 'Daddy is serious. You better go back, show him what you're made of, and stop crying.'

"I followed her, step by step, until she reached the porch. She slowly raised her thin arm up to show him her brick. Standing on the porch, looking down at the two of us, he said, '*That* is a brick.' Pointing to the edge of the porch, he told us to sit down.

"Michael, check this shit out. My dad's blue-hazel eyes seemed change colors with his mood. Blue meant everything was good, green meant he wasn't happy with you and was fighting-mad. His green eyes were glued on Lily as he told her, 'I want you to hold that brick and think about what you will do with it the next time someone passes the first lick. Baby, I am tired of you running home crying.' Then he turned and walked back into the house.

"Putting my arm around her shoulders, I said, 'You need to defend yourself. Stop letting people bully you. I will fight for you, but keep in mind, I can't do it forever.' Just as I finished talking to her, Daddy came back with three popsicles. For a moment, I thought he was going over to Pudding's house demanding an apology, but knowing how mad he was, that was so far from the truth.

"He sat between the two of us and handed out the treats. While tearing open his popsicle cover, he said, 'Babies, you know how much I love the both of you. I know it might seem like I'm being mean, but I'm not. I want my queens to be independent, smart, and fearless. Lily, it breaks my heart to see you so afraid that you can't even fight for yourself.'

"Before he started on his popsicle, he gave us both a hug and kissed us on top of our heads. 'If I could, I would fight all of y'all's battles—but I can't, and I won't,' he said.

"We finished our popsicles in silence and continued to sit on the porch with Daddy while swinging our legs. Lily was still holding her brick. Daddy broke the silence when he jumped off the porch, turned around, and collected the popsicle wrappers and sticks. Slowly, he moved the white towel on his shoulder from the left to the right side, looked down, and told Lily, 'Let this be the last time you come home beat up. Sit there and hold that brick. I want you to show me what you'll do if someone bothers you again. Don't worry about the grown-ups . . . I can handle them.'

"Daddy headed back into the house. I did not hear the screen door open. I could still smell his cologne. Then I heard him say my name, and before I could turn around, he said, 'Don't go out looking for a fight.'

"But the only thing on my mind was teaching Pudding a lesson about bullying my sister. After all, he said not to go *looking* for a fight. He never said *don't* fight for my sister. Big difference. I scanned the backyard until my eyes locked on the fading-red metal slide next to the swing set and how it could easily topple over. I thought about moving it next to the large briar patch and the ant bed next to the slide. I thought about Lily's brick.

"While my parents were away, I dragged the slide closer to the briar patch with the huge thorns and the large ant bed, placed Lily's brick on the seat of the swing next to the slide, and then I waited.

"Finally, one day, I looked out the window, and like an eagle watching its prey . . . Michael, guess who I saw."

"Was it Pudding?" Michael asked.

"You got it," I said. "Pudding was outside acting like she didn't make my sister cry, like she was welcome to play in our yard, like I wasn't my big sister's little sister. When Pudding saw me, she took off running. Just as she reached her yard, I called for her to come back over to play jack stones.

"We sat there, tossing the worn metal jacks on the back of our hands while throwing the red ball in the air. After the game, I said, 'Want a popsicle?'"

"Joy, wait. 'Want a popsicle?'" Michael laughed.

"Girl, yes, my crazy behind offered her a popsicle, and of course her greedy ass said, 'Sure.' I told her we had two yellow ones left, and I had to save one for my sister. I ran into the house, grabbed our popsicles, and placed them in my mouth, laughing. When I got outside, I put the popsicles in the white cooler next to the door and suggested we get on the slide before we snacked. As she walked to the set, all I could think about was my sister when she held that dirty, cement-covered brick—her messed-up hair, that one shoe.

"Pudding climbed to the top of the slide, and in my mind, I could feel my sister's tears. In the middle of her climb, Pudding made me promise not to let go of the ladder. I reassured her, 'Don't worry, I'm holding it.'

"When she got to the top, she slowly sat down, holding the rails. As she sat there, I began to shake the slide, focusing on the sound of that slide hitting the ground and Pudding's cries from landing dead center into that briar patch.

"As she lay there, I got Lily's brick, stood over Pudding, and said, 'This is what you get for bullying my sister.' I threw the brick down, walked away, grabbed both popsicles out of the white cooler, and went back into the house.

"By the time my dad pulled up, you could tell by the way he opened the car door he'd noticed the downed slide. On his way to fix it, he stopped dead in his tracks. I knew he was standing dead center in the briar patch. I'm not sure what hit him first, the thorns or the ants, but suddenly—in a flash—he dropped the slide and frantically smacked his legs. I ran out to help, but I knew not to get too close to the slide."

"Joy, hold up, you didn't warn him?" said Michael.

"Hell, no! I was smart enough to just let him figure it out. Now, stop interrupting me. Let me finish the damn story."

"I'll keep quiet," said Michael, "but Joy, you better not be making some shit up."

"Baby girl, trust me, I'm not. Back to my story. Now, in the middle of all this, I could see three figures charging like a herd of angry elephants toward our yard. From a distance, I heard, 'Hey, Red!'

"My dad turned in the voice's direction. Pudding, her toothless mama, Lucille, and her skinny, drunk papa, Leroy, were standing at the edge of our property. They weren't so out of control or pissed that they would dare cross into our territory. I stood by my dad's side, and Pudding stood by her mama's side.

"Before her mama opened her mouth, my dad shut her down. He said, 'Look, I do not appreciate your daughter mistreating my daughter, and Lily has my permission to knock Pudding out with a brick the next time she wants to fight.' Then he turned and just walked away, never giving Mrs. Lucille time to explain why she was ready for battle. When we got back to the carport, my daddy was sitting like a proud lion—legs crossed and with a cigarette in mouth. He proudly said, 'Family, I knew Lily had kick-ass in her veins.'

"No one had the heart to tell him what really happened. You know damn well *I* didn't. Well, thirty years later, guess who was standing behind me in the grocery store check-out?"

With a faint response, Michael guessed, "Pudding!"

"Yep, Pudding. At first, she tried to act like she didn't recognize me. Looking in her eyes, all I said was,

'Hi.' Trying to look cute, I guess, she said 'Hi, I think I know you. Are you from Miami?'

"I knew she remembered that red slide. Smiling, I replied, 'Girl, bless your heart,' Now, in the South, this is *not* a compliment. 'You remember me.' With a shit-eating smile on her face, she said, 'Yes, yes. I remember you. Joy, you look great. How is Lily?' Michael, did she just ask me how *my freaking sister was doing*?

"Looking at her jacked-up weave, I wanted to ask her how she trained that cat to sit still on the top of her head. She bullied my sister for her lovely flowing curls, and now she was looking like a damn clown with that curly cat weave. It made me so hot, I wanted to snatch it off. So, smiling, I replied, 'Girl, she is still being sweet Lily.'

"We stood there. She looked like a hot mess, and I was thinking, *What the total fuck?* Once we finished our fake conversation, she moved on and I thought about how I got her back for making my sister cry."

Laughing until she choked, Michael screamed, "You have been crazy all your life!"

"Damn real. I will fight for me and mine. So, Michael, the point is, I'm not telling you to go to jail for assault, but I think you got the moral of the story. I tell you the truth—it is a bitch being me, but I love myself way too much to allow anyone or anything to keep me in bound with fear. You might as well be a slave on some fool's plantation.

"Look, all I'm saying is, do not be a slave to your fears or your 'monkey mind.' All your joy is standing behind your fears, calling you to free the monkey in your mind and meet the better you. Fight for yourself, fight for what you stand for, and fight through your fears."

"Wow, I never thought about it like that. You make it look so easy," Michael said.

"Baby, it looks easy, but it is not. It is a process. I freed my monkey mind early in life and I have been fearless ever since." I took a deep breath. "Michael, let what I shared soak in. Now, let's have happy talk. How's your catering business going?"

"Everything's going great. I've secured several catering contracts with some of the judges and lawyers that Darren work with, and am catering several company and movie events this month."

"That's great!" I said.

"You know, I never thought my passion would turn into one of my proudest accomplishments. Cooking and entertaining have always been my passion. After marrying Darren, he wanted me to stop working. His take was his daddy always provided and his mom never worked. I'm sure it worked for her—since she never liked working—but for me, there is nothing like making your own money and having fun at the same time."

"What made you get started?" I asked.

"To give credit where it is due, it was Donna's idea. You know, my old housekeeper. While she cleaned, I would make sure I prepared her lunch. She would always encourage me to turn my passion into a business. I knew opening a restaurant was not what I wanted, so I started thinking about catering. When my catering business picked up, I hired Donna's sister to do the housekeeping and I hired Donna to help with the business. I felt good being able to give her sister a job and to give Donna an opportunity to have full employment with benefits."

I said, "I am so proud of how your business is taking off. Michael, I'm not going to hold you up, but I want you to just think about what we discussed. Gypsy's going out of town Friday. Let's get together, just you and me. My calendar is open, so connect with me later on with the details."

Holding back what sounded like tears, she said, "Joy, thanks so much for being you. Love you. I'll text you the details later."

"Okay. Love you back. Stay your beautiful self."

CHAPTER 10

PULL BACK

Joy

I needed to hurry to make my eleven o'clock appointment with this therapist. I took Gypsy's advice to check out my "hyper nature," and, well, to be honest with myself, it really came about after last week's altercation with one of my old "bed buddies."

Let's call him Mr. Thang.

I cannot believe this five-foot-six trick came over all jacked up, acting taller than he really was. Let me just take you back to why Mr. Thang had to "keep it moving." He fell back in love with his white girl and loved her more than he loved me.

Now, I know what some might think when I say "white girl." I'm not talking about the lovely white sistas with hearts of gold. I'm talking about his love for his other white girl—cocaine.

When he was high, I would say he was "girled up." He had it so bad, if he had to travel out of town, he would take the grip off his golf clubs and hide his coke inside. I told him if he ever got caught, I was going to leave him at the airport.

I went against my number-one rule: do not go back to the same rabid dog to be bit again in the same wound. But I guess rules are made to be broken, and hell if I know why I chose this one.

We started dating again for about two months. I thought it would be better not to share the reunion with my girls. I wanted to give him another chance to correct himself and then introduce the "new him." After looking back, I was just as crazy as he still was.

Well, I guess nothing changed but his drug contact. I noticed the little tell-tale signs: first, the sudden sinus issues and being irritable, then running late or missing scheduled dates, having to run off for a minute, but—most important—the change in his sexual performance and desires.

When he was all "girled up," his first thing was to cross-dress and walk around the house like he was on the TV show *Dynasty*. I mean in an old, ugly Aunt Esther wig, heels, and black fishnet stockings, with the desire to get dog-fucked by some thug boy. But when he wasn't high, he swore he was straight. What pissed me off though was he had the *nerve* to make a comment about my gay cousin.

Is that not some special shit?

Back to why I'm heading to the therapist. Mr. Thang came over all high, and I guess he had a streak of lunacy. I picked up his phone—okay, okay, I was *checking* his phone—and before I knew what hit me, he tackled me to the floor and grabbed his phone. While lying flat on my back with this *What the total fuck?* look on my face, he had the nerve to look down at me with a cheap half-smile and then just walk off to the bathroom.

After I got up off the floor and examined my body, I

saw these large black and blue bruises all over my arms and legs reminding me of old Junior Korn. Something in me snapped.

I walked to the bathroom to find him taking a piss. When he realized I was standing there, he looked out the corner of his eye and just looked back down into the toilet like, *You asked for that attack.*

Before I knew it, I walked up and jabbed him right smack in his left ear, and with the next punch, I hit him right in the eye. I guess the punch combination from my tomboy days still worked, because while still holding his dick Mr. Thang fell back into the shower and—like my old country uncles used to say—he hit the floor like a sack of taters. You could see the trail of pee from the back of the toilet, up the wall, across the ceiling, and finishing up in the tub. The funniest thing was, when he landed in the shower, he was mindful enough to keep holding his dick. Once I saw he was wrapped up in the shower curtain, I had the mind to continue with what he asked for, but something in me screamed, *Stop and pull back!*

So, that's what I did.

I just walked away and locked myself in my bedroom. I stayed there for about thirty minutes, and when I came out, he was still lying on the bathroom floor. *Now* I wasn't done with him.

I went to the garage and threw his work PC, clothes, and cocaine in a large trash can, topping it off with some used kitty litter, and sat it out in the rain. I ran back into the house and made him get up and out.

Once he realized what I'd done, he said he was going to call the cops. I handed him my phone and told him, "Call. Keep in mind, I'm going to work you over until they get here."

Maybe he thought about how he was all "girled up" and I was covered with bruises, and he changed his burned-out mind.

"Just in case you want to get cute after you leave here, try me." I showed him pictures of him in drag.

I guess I was fooling myself. I left him and the situation alone, but I knew I needed to address my anger-management issues.

The traffic was, as usual, horrible. I only had to drive twenty miles, but based on what I knew about Atlanta traffic, it would take me the traditional forty-five minutes.

Finally, I made it with time to spare. I saw plenty of open parking spaces up front. Since I was trying to stay fit, I parked as far away as possible and enjoyed the sunshine as I walked in. You know I love the full-figure girls, but it kills me to see a four-hundred-pound sista looking flawless, hair done, feet and nails done, with eyelashes that look like live butterflies, but her body so unhealthy.

Oh, well, not my business, so let me just keep my focus on myself.

At the receptionist counter, the lady asked if she could help me. With my smart mouth and a big smile, I replied, "I sure hope so." She didn't smile, so I introduced myself, signed in, and slowly turned around, looking for a good seat. I found an interesting magazine about healthy cooking right on top of a gun and hunting magazine. I must say their literature selection was quite interesting.

With the magazine face down, I read it from the back to the front, as usual. I've done it that way all my life. I should have known that something was wrong with me.

As soon as I got into an article, the nurse called me to the back, so I picked up my purse and magazine, and followed the nurse down a long, sterile hallway ending with these massive French doors with Dr. Sheeley's name on one door and WELCOME on the other.

The nurse opened the door up into a gorgeous office with the most beautiful mural behind the sofa. She pointed to the sofa and told me to take a seat. The office smelled of fresh flowers, and soft jazz was playing in the background. As she walked out, I noticed tons of things for me to go through before Dr. Sheeley came in. I hate to admit this, but every time I go to the doctor, I get a kick out of going through the drawers in exam rooms. I never knew what I was looking for, but it was fun.

I wasn't sure if it would be a good idea to treat his personal office like an exam room, so I just walked around and looked at his pictures and awards. While I had my back turned, admiring the garden view, the door swung open, and a fine, tall, dark, handsome man walked in, smiling and smelling like goodness. He reached out and shook my hand, and I knew we would be a perfect team.

I sat on a soft aqua-blue sofa, and he sat in the large chair slightly in front of me. He opened the session by asking me what my motivation for coming in was. From there, he moved to asking me more lifestyle questions, dating, drinking, and of course, he touched on my childhood.

He asked me to talk a little about my messes and ex-thangs, so the first one to come to mind of course was Mess Number Three. I shared with him my naming convention. As I started talking about the messes, I had to get up and move around. Sitting does not give me the vantage point when I start down memory lane.

With his most soothing voice, he asked me, "Do you have any thoughts of hurting yourself or others?"

I had to pause before answering. My reply was typical

me. "I love me, life, and living too much to hurt myself, and I do not have any active thoughts of hurting anyone else. Per my lifestyle, I have been married six times, and I am currently dating. As far as my drinking, I usually drink about two glasses of wine every night."

Dr. Sheeley said, "First, Ms. Holmes, since you have been in here, you have moved every item on my desk—not sure why you had to look under the statues—and you constantly were in motion, not to mention you never completed one topic before moving to the next. Based on what you've shared and my observation, my early diagnosis is a mild case of ADHD, attention-deficit/hyperactivity disorder. However, I think we need a couple of follow-up sessions for me to give you a final diagnosis and to map out the best way to help you manage."

When he finished, I told him, "I always knew something was a little special about me. During my childhood, my teachers complained to my parents about my 'daydreaming' and my short attention span. Funny, it was suggested to my parents I should be placed in the special-education class, but keep in mind I was a straight-A student and one year ahead of my class. When we need something to talk about, I'll give you the R-rated response my mother gave to the teacher."

Dr. Sheeley said, "Tell me about it."

"Do I have to tell the entire story?"

"Ms. Holmes, I need you to open up and tell me the entire story," he replied.

I took a deep breath and began. "My first- and second-grade teacher was Ms. Smith, a small, bitter soul. On the first day of school, Ms. Smith went around the room and had us stand up, tell our name, our parents' names, and where our parents worked. When it was my turn, I stood up and said, 'My mother's name is Sandra Holmes, and my daddy's name is Red.'

"Before I could say another word, Ms. Smith said, '*What is your daddy's name?*' I said, 'Red.' After the second try, she just moved on.

"That evening, just as Mama asked how my day was at dinner, the phone rang. From the conversation, I knew it was Ms. Smith. They talked for a couple of minutes, and when my mom came back to the table, she had this look on her face like she was about to die with laughter.

"My big sister, Lily, and I both looked at her like, 'What? What?' Then she looked at me and asked, 'What is your daddy's name?'

"I said, 'Red.'

"My sister dropped her fork, with a look that said she was wondering what she missed and how she'd failed. Then Lily said, 'Girl, that is not his real name.'

"I said, 'Yes, it is.'

"Lily said, 'That is what everyone calls him, but his real name is Walter Holmes Sr.'

"The table was completely quiet. Then we all broke out laughing.

"Back in the day, teachers could punish the students. Now, other teachers would have you hold out your hand and use that light-brown ruler with the metal strip. Not Ms. Smith. She would try to break our backs with a paddle that looked like some weapon she made and decorated while she was a slave.

One day, she told me before recess that she wanted me to clean the erasers. When the bell rang, all the kids ran out for a quick play, and I walked up to her desk. She sat there acting like she was reading. I guess she thought I was heading to the blackboard, but I ended up at the front of her wooden desk. 'Excuse me, Ms. Smith, the chalk makes my throat dry, so I can't clean the board nor the erasers.'

"Slowly Ms. Smith reached up, and without raising her head, took off her glasses. 'Repeat what you just said,' she told me. So, I said it again. Without warning, she jumped up. 'If you do not do as you are told, I'm going to call your mother tonight.'

"To her surprise, I stepped back, turned around, and went outside to play with the other kids. While I was playing tag, I saw my mother sitting outside with her class. I waved my hands to get her attention. She did not see me, but one of her students told her to look in my direction. She waved for me to come to the edge of the playground.

"As we walked toward each other, she looked concerned. She said, 'What's wrong? Why aren't you playing with the other kids?'

"I told her about Ms. Smith, and that she was going to call her tonight. Then, dropping my head, I whispered to Mama, 'I am so sorry for being hard-headed, but you know the chalk makes me sick.'

"Standing there in the sun, sweating like I just played hopscotch, I heard her fumbling around in her purse. When she stopped, I felt a tissue wipe my face, and then she gave me a piece of peppermint, told me to eat it, and to go back and play. On my way back to class, I could see Ms. Smith outside standing in the sun, surrounded by a cloud of white dust. Ms. Smith never called, and my mama left it alone.

"Now, let's get to that paddle. Ms. Smith found every opportunity to bring me to the front of the class for my daily paddling. No lie, she beat me every day, other than Saturdays, Sundays, and holidays.

"During class one day, we were talking about boats. I

proudly shared with the class that my daddy was a longshoreman. When I said that, Ms. Smith looked like she just drank a big glass of vinegar and—all at once—pieces fell in place. I had a clear vision of why I was always in her crosshairs. It explained why she hated my existence.

"After dinner, my sister and I were cleaning up the dinner dishes, and my mama was sitting on the sofa, checking papers. When she was done, she got up, and on her way to her room she reminded us to sweep the kitchen and told us we could have a slice of chocolate cake after our baths. By that time, we were wrapping up the kitchen. My sister told me to go take my bath, and she would finish up. On my way to the to the bathroom, the phone rang.

"While I was in the bathroom, my sister came in and closed the door. 'Girl, you are in trouble. What have you done?'

"I couldn't think of anything, so I said, 'Done? Like what?'

"Lily said, 'I think Mama is talking to Ms. Smith, and I mean it is freaking heated.' Then she said, 'Let me see if I can hear more.' With her back turned, she slowly opened the door, stuck her head out, and eased back into the kitchen.

"After my bath, I went back into the kitchen for my cake. My mother's papers were still on the sofa, and her door was still closed. Suddenly, the door flew open and Mama came out, visibly upset. I could hear her talking under her breath, but she just went back to checking her papers. Suddenly I heard, 'Joy.'

"I was too scared to turn around, so I said 'Yes?' to my cake.

"'Make sure you brush your teeth before you go to bed.'

"I thought it was a trick. But suddenly, I heard her

getting up. Looking out the corner of my eye, I saw her just standing there, still upset, then she just walked up to me and gave me a big hug. Now, I was confused, but I just let it go.

"After that night, Ms. Smith beat me just for the wind blowing. One day, I came to school with this cute short set and matching sandals. During lunch, one of the little girls complimented me. I told her my daddy picked it out. When I said that, Ms. Smith popped her head up and just stared at me. Her reaction confirmed what I had been thinking.

"At dinner, I stopped in the middle of eating my corn on the cob. I turned to Mama and out of the blue asked her, 'Was Daddy ever married to Ms. Smith?'

"My sister chimed in, 'Where did you get that madness from? Daddy likes *pretty* women, and she is much older than he is.'

"My mom was still looking at me, mouth open, grasping her glass. She was just holding it. She never picked the glass up. She said, 'Yes—how did you know that?'

"Now my sister's mouth opened and she was grasping her glass.

"Then Mama said, 'Why do you ask?'

"I started to tell her how Ms. Smith treated me and how she would paddle me for no reason at all. Looking at her with tears running down my face, I said, 'Every time I mention my daddy, she finds a reason to punish me.' My head dropped and tears just started to drip, one by one, all over my corn.

"Suddenly, I felt my mama pulling my ponytail, just like my daddy. When I looked up, she had tears in her eyes. I guess my soft tears showed her I had been tormented. Suddenly, she started biting her lip, and tears just rolled down her face.

"We heard a knock at the door. My mama slid her chair back and proceeded to the door. After clearing her throat, she asked who it was.

"'Sandra, this is Ms. Smith. I dropped by to talk to you about Joy.'

"Now, I can't make this up. My blood boiled. My sister looked at me looking at her. As the door opened, our heads turned at the same time. Mama welcomed her in, offered her a seat, and sent us to our bedrooms. Can I tell you, as soon as my sister partially closed the door, all hell broke loose? The only voice I heard was my mom's. She told Ms. Smith she would break her neck if she bothered me again.

"Then I heard something else that messed me up. My mom told Ms. Smith, 'I didn't appreciate you calling last week suggesting we place Joy in Special Ed. There is not a damn thing wrong with my child.'

"Now, keep in mind I was a grade ahead, and I had good grades. Walking away from the door, I told my sister about it. Suddenly, I heard my mom call me. I opened the door slowly and, with my sister leading the way, we walked into the den. We saw Ms. Smith in tears. My mom stood up, walked over, and pulled me close to her. She turned and told Ms. Smith, 'You place your hands on my child, I will kick your ass.' Looking at her from head to toe, she followed up with, 'It is a cotton-picking shame you would mistreat a child because you can't get over her dad.'

"Before my mother finished, there was another knock on the door. This time it was my Uncle Sonny from next door. My mom let him in.

"My uncle, looking confused, said, 'What's going on? I can't believe what I just heard. You know the window is open.' Standing in front of my mom, he told her, 'Step outside so you can cool off.' Slowly, Mama walked toward the door. My uncle escorted her outside and closed the door behind her.

"Then, looking at Ms. Smith, he asked, 'Have you lost your damn mind? Now, let me set you straight. You will *not* harass my brother's children. I know you—I know you well. Please don't try me. Lord knows she is a little bad ass, but her little bad ass is a member of the Holmes family. Remember that.'

"I stood there looking at her looking at him, saying nothing. Ms. Smith got the hell out of there, and my uncle followed. Once they were outside, my sister and I ran to the window. All we could see was my uncle holding the car door open and my mom standing in front of the car looking like she was about to jump on the hood.

"My mom come back in, then we heard Ms. Smith pull out the drive, lights off and burning rubber. My uncle didn't come back in the house. My mom went into her room and slammed the door. My sister and I grabbed two yellow popsicles and started watching *Good Times* like nothing happened.

"The next day, my uncle came over with my favorite homemade jelly cake. To this day, they never uttered a word about that night—not Ms. Smith, my sister, my mom, or my uncle. But you know, I told my dad."

When I finished, I asked Dr. Sheeley, "Let me ask you this. What causes ADHD?"

Turning to his desk, Dr. Sheeley pulled out a pamphlet explaining ADHD. While he passed me the pamphlet, he said, "Experts don't really know exactly what causes ADHD. Some believe genes may play an important role in who develops ADHD, and some believe it could be environmental issues, such as exposure to cigarettes, alcohol, or other toxins while in the womb.

"However, unlike other psychiatric disorders, ADHD doesn't begin in adulthood. There are always some symptoms present in childhood. You overcame it in your childhood, and it seems you are managing it as an adult, but I feel you need to spend time on your anger-management issues.

"Ms. Holmes, I would like to see you next week, so schedule a time with the receptionist." Pausing for a minute, he added, "You have a lovely personality. I am looking forward to our next session."

CHAPTER 11

GIVING BACK

Gypsy

I think it's time for a little payback. Joy is always playing on the phone.
 I called her from my work phone. When she picked up, using my best "Get it, Girl" voice, I said, "Hey, skank, I saw you out with my man."
 You could hear complete silence, and then I just started laughing my head off. "See how it feels to be the butt of some crazy shit?"
 Joy started screaming at the top of her lungs, "See, that is why I hate you! I was about to light you up. What's up? I stopped by your house, but I saw the light on in your spare room, so I knew you were out of town."
 "Yes, ma'am, that's why I'm calling you. Look, I need to go check on my grandparents. I got a strange call from my Aunt Betty, so I thought it was time for me to go home. I really need to put my eyes on them. Let Michael know, and please keep an eye on her while I'm gone. I hate to tell you this, but I think you're right about Skutch. So, if he

pops off, call me. You both have the keys to the house if she needs some place to chill out. Damn, I'm talking like you."

In a very serious tone, the only thing Joy said was, "Will do."

Driving down to Waycross, Georgia, is always fun. The I-75 South traffic is crazy, especially around McDonough. Cruising off I-75 South onto US-82 East, I stopped at the gas station to use the bathroom and gas up.

On my way out of Tifton, I noticed the sign: WAYCROSS: 65 MILES. I knew damn well that sign was wrong. Sixty-five miles to go at sixty-five miles an hour should take me one hour. Wrong. It never fails. It takes an hour and thirty minutes, hands down.

Damn, Joy's calling me again. I hope everything's okay. I better pick up. "Hey, what's up?"

"Nothing, girl. I was just checking on you. I tried to call earlier, and when you didn't pick up, I was a little worried. You know, you and Michael are my only friends, and I want to make sure you are okay."

Not to sound stressed, I said, "All is good. I am just going to check on my folks. The call from my aunt made me think something wasn't right with them, so I decided at the last minute to ride down. Remember I shared with you how all my folks came through for me when I had my boys?"

Angrily, Joy said, "You mean when you were raped, and your parents didn't believe you, so they shipped you off to the country? You bet I remember. You said your folks down in Waycross were really good to you."

"Correct. Now that my folks are getting older, it seems like they are becoming a little needy, and some of their kids are all about themselves. My aunt did not sound like herself. I fear she has dementia. Funny, she'll call me before she calls her kids.

"Joy, I better slow down going through these small towns. Most of them are speed traps. Look, let me call you back when I get there."

Joy said, "Okay, no worries. Remind me to tell you something funny the next time we talk."

I saw the Ware County sign. I thought I'd better stop by my aunt's house first. I thought she needed for me to love on her. I'd call my grandparents later.

Lord, all the stop signs and railroad tracks. I don't know why she moved so far back in the woods.

As soon as I pulled up, I saw Big Daddy's truck. Now I was worried. You can't catch my grandparents out of the house after dark. Jumping out of the car, I ran up on the porch right into Big Daddy's arms. With his arms around, he said, "Baby, I am so glad you are here."

"What happened?"

"We have been trying to get Aunt Betty to move in with us. She really does not need to be out here alone."

I thought to myself, *Lord, the blind leading the deaf.*

"Sadly, she wants to stay here so her kids can have a home to come back to."

I said, "Her kids haven't been here for over five years!"

Big Daddy said, "Gypsy, we got a call from the police telling us to come pick her up from the gas station ten miles outside of town. She said she was going to work and got lost." Big Daddy started to cry. "You know she has not worked in ten years. It's so sad. Now, baby, that isn't the only thing. When we got here, the house was a mess—everything is all over the floor, and she has all her mail in the oven."

I held Big Daddy's hand and kissed it. I reassured him,

"Everything is going to be okay, and I will stay as long as you need me. Hold your head up, Big Daddy, and stop crying."

Funny—I remember him telling me the same when I was pregnant.

I told him to stay on the porch; I wanted to talk to her alone. As soon as I walked in, Aunt Betty started crying like a baby and said, "I knew you would come to take care of me."

I hugged her real tight and asked her to come with me to my grandparents'. She agreed, and I told Big Daddy to take her home and I would lock up her house.

Looking around after everyone left just broke my heart. Aunt Betty always kept an orderly home, and now it looked like a locker room.

Let me check her mail. Damn, all her bills are past due, and she has a water shut-off notice. I better take care of this first thing in the morning; based on this letter they'll turn her water off next Monday.

Now, what the hell is this? Please tell me this is not right. She has two cash withdrawals over ten thousand dollars apiece! What does she need that much money for? Her house and car are paid for. I better have a talk with her first thing in the morning. But for now, I will just lock up and come back with her and my grandparents tomorrow.

Driving down the long gravel road up to my grandparents', I saw their large plantation-like house sitting at the end of the drive. I could never remember *not* having the pond that sat out front. The county would come out every so often to stock the pond, and as kids we enjoyed fishing off the old dock.

I noticed someone had rebuilt that dock recently. I remembered how, during the summer, the boys would go out and fish all day, and at night family would cook the fish in the yard over a fire in this large black wash pot that had been in the family since slavery.

Big Mama's twin sister, Granny, married Big Daddy's twin brother, Granddaddy. Funny, the twins never lived off the farm. Their homes were connected by a long breezeway. In front, there was a large wraparound porch with white rocking chairs and two swings hanging from the wood-plank ceiling. Every weekend, the old folk would sit on the porch, and the kids would use the breezeway as their hangout spot.

Behind the house was a ten-acre garden with a large chicken pen. We kids all stayed on the farm every summer, and every summer we picked vegetables and helped prep them for freezing and canning. I still get chills and my thumbs hurt every time I see a large wash pan next to a wood hamper full of beans. When we complained, my aunties would say, "You don't complain when they're on your plate."

With my child-mind, I thought, *What the hell does that have to do with my thumbs?* I never understood why they wouldn't just go buy this from the grocery store like my friends at school. Nowadays, Big Mama and Big Daddy pay for help to maintain the garden and help with the canning. And yes, they still have their chickens.

I was at ease seeing Big Daddy's truck. It took a load off my mind knowing all the old folk were under one roof, and I was there to watch over them.

As soon as I walked in, Big Mama came out of the kitchen like always, wiping her hands on that white apron. Other than her church clothes, I really don't know what the front of her dresses look like. I think she uses that apron as her shield of honor. It shows that she is always ready to feed her family's body, soul, and mind.

Before Big Mama made it out of the kitchen, her identical twin, Granny, was right behind her. Funny, she always wore a half apron that tied around her waist, and Big Mama always wore a full apron that tied around her waist and around her neck. Either way, they both matched. As identical twins, I guess you never grow out of dressing alike.

Big Mama said, "Your boys were down for a week last month."

Granny chimed in, "They did a health fair at the church. You know some folk can't afford to go to the doctor, so those two bring the doctor to us."

Looking in my eyes, Big Mama said, "Those boys are angels from heaven. God never makes a mistake."

After dinner, I went out on the front porch to collect my thoughts. *I have a good life in Atlanta, but I need to take time to come back and set everyone straight.*

Aunt Betty was heavy on my mind, and I had to bring myself together to call her kids; I needed to make sure I kept my cool and selected my words. Thank God, no one answered, and I didn't leave a message. They act like their mother's dead. When my auntie had breast cancer, none of her kids came down to check on her. At that point, she gave me power of attorney and put all that she owned in my name rather than in theirs.

So, the first thing I needed to do in the morning was go to the bank and figure out what was up with her money. I guessed I was going to have to either cancel my plans for the country retreat or change the scope.

Let me pray on it. I know God will guide my steps.

CHAPTER 12

UP AND OUT

Gypsy

There's nothing like waking up to my grandparents singing and the smell of homemade biscuits. Funny, my grandparents have always been health conscious; they never ate pork or beef, but plenty of chicken, turkey, and fish.

When I was a young, I would always tell them, "A chicken would be proud to enter your kitchens." So, I knew what the menu would be: grits, homemade chicken sausage, fresh eggs, tomatoes, and those homemade biscuits.

As I started for the kitchen, I heard the screen door close. Big Mama came in with a large white bowl full of brown eggs. She looked up and said, "Sit down and let me fix your plate."

I asked, "Do you want me to call Big Daddy and Grand Daddy?"

"You know they already ate, but go get your granny. She wanted to join us for breakfast."

Just as I was about to get up, Granny came in with a

large tray pies. She sat them in the middle of the table while Big Mama made coffee. After we said grace, I told them about my plans for the day. "I need to go to the bank to sort out Aunt Betty's account."

I felt them looking at me as I ate. Granny broke the ice and asked, "So, where are you with your retreat? Are you still planning on building it on Papa's place?"

Not looking up, I said, "That was the plan, but I am having second thoughts. After dealing with Aunt Betty, I'm thinking about holding off or maybe changing from a retreat to a retirement home. Lord, there are enough of us to keep the home full."

Everyone chuckled.

When I was about to leave for the bank, Big Mama came out of the kitchen with a fresh cup of coffee and a bag full of fried pies. "These are for you to take back to Atlanta. Put them in the freezer—they will travel better frozen. Make sure you share with Joy and Michael."

On my way to the freezer, I told her, "I'm not sharing. They will have to come down to get their own."

Tapping the back of my hand, Big Mama said, "Baby, you know you can't eat all of those pies. Give my girls at least one." Then, looking concerned for me, she kissed me and told me, "Just watch God. Before you finish your day, God will show you the way. Just continue to pray."

I drove the truck instead of my car; something about driving an old pickup down those country roads clears my head and heart. As soon as I pulled out, I saw Big Daddy and Granddaddy walking around the pond. Since I was a little girl, my grands got up every morning and walked at least two miles a day. They used to say, "Start your day out with Mother Nature. You are never too old to have your mother wash your face with a little sunshine."

When I got to town, I was able to park in front of the bank. I turned the engine off, sat, and whispered a prayer: "God, please guide my steps, show me the truth, and help me understand what is in front of me. Amen."

On my way to the bank, I ran into my Uncle Ed, Big Mama's youngest brother. "How is my little princess?" he asked.

Like I did when I was little, I wanted to fall into his arms and cry like a baby, but instead, I said, "Hi, Uncle Ed. Your little princess is okay, I think. I'm going back out to the farm. Please meet me out there in about an hour. I'll give you an update when we connect."

Hugging me, he said, "Funny, I'm on my way out there now." Then, just like he did when I was a child, he pulled out his wallet and gave me two dollars. He said, "Baby, go by your cousin's ice cream parlor and treat yourself."

I had to try harder not to cry when he handed me the money. "I guess I'm always a little princess in your eyes."

I watched him walk off until he turned the corner. Suddenly my tears just started to flow, thinking about how loving our family is.

After I got myself together, I walked inside the bank. Just as the door closed, the bank manager greeted me with a lovely smile. "Morning! Welcome. How can I help you?"

"Hello, my name is Gypsy Hunt. I need to talk to someone concerning questionable account activities."

The bank manager introduced himself as Peter, then asked me to sign in and follow him. "Now, Ms. Hunt, may I please have your account information?"

I handed him my ID as he turned to his computer and pulled up my account. Looking up from the computer, Peter said, "I see you are the primary owner of this account and Ms. Betty Hunt is joint owner of the account."

"Yes, that is correct." Then I shared with him my concern around the account activity and asked if he could walk me through the account history.

Looking at the account information, Peter said, "Let me print the history and give you some time to review."

My heart started to sink after five pages were printed. Pushing his chair back, he handed me the printout and a yellow marker. "Please highlight any transactions that you have concerns about."

When he said that, my heart beat fast, then I wanted to just throw up. *The only activity on Aunt Betty's account should be her monthly retirement deposits.* When I reached out, he could see my hands shaking.

Before leaving the room, Peter asked, "Ms. Hunt, are you going to be okay?"

Trying not to react to the first transaction on the account, I whispered, "Yes, sir, thank you for asking." *The receiver of this transaction was to Aunt Betty's crackhead son Charles. Knowing him, I'm pretty sure he was behind the other transactions.*

After Peter left, I muttered, "What the hell am I looking at? If Charles was in the room, I would kick his stank ass!"

The first transaction was ten thousand dollars directly deposited to Charles' checking account. The second and third transactions went to another account. Together, they totaled over thirty thousand dollars. The rest of the transactions were small amounts, between fifty to one hundred dollars, to a different account. Instead of highlighting each transaction, I made a big X across all the pages. Then, pushing the papers away from me, I threw the highlighter to the floor and laid my head down on the desk. I did not have the strength to get up to let Peter know I was done.

How could this happen? I placed an alert on this account so that any transaction over a hundred dollars needs to be approved by me, and I placed a forty-dollar-a-day limit on her cash withdrawals!

Thank God I kept all my papers concerning this account. Thumbing through them, I found the paperwork where I set the alert and limits. Now, I was freaking mad at Charles *and* the damn bank.

Hell, this is not my problem. I know one damn thing: they better put all her money back.

Peter knocked on the door before coming in. "Ms. Hunt, are you done?"

I wanted to stand on the top of his desk and scream, "FUCK NO!" Instead, I told him, "I think you all have an issue. Please come in. Let me show you what I found, and let me share what I have." Handing him the marked-up printout, I told him all the transactions that were over one hundred dollars were fraudulent, and the ones that went to Charles' accounts were questionable.

After looking at my markups, he looked at me and asked, "Are you sure?"

"Yes," I said, then handed him the form where I placed the alerts and the limits.

When he reached out, I could see his hands shaking like a leaf.

Reaching for my bag, I told him I expected to have *all* this money back in her account by the end of the day. Standing and looking him straight in his eyes, I said, "This should not have happened. Not my problem. I will call you tomorrow. Have a good day." Then I walked out, feeling better but pissed.

Thinking about Uncle Ed, I walked down to the ice cream parlor, ordered some ice cream, and paid for it with my two dollars that he gave me.

After, I headed to the farm. Driving home, every lick of ice cream seemed to take away my frustration.

When I got to the farm, Uncle Ed and the rest of my family were sitting on the porch—including Aunt Betty. While I gathered all my papers, Uncle Ed opened my car door. "Princess, how's your day?"

I handed him my empty ice cream bag, and he said, "Look at my princess. I know you're feeling better."

"Yep, thanks! Listen, I was able to work everything out."

After giving him the details, I saw Big Mama standing with her hands on her hips. She yelled out, "Ed, let the child come up to the house."

As we walked, I told him, "See if you can get Aunt Betty off the porch. I don't want her to hear me tell everyone how low-down her brat is right now."

Holding my hand, he replied, "Will do, princess. I think that's a good idea."

When we got to the porch, Uncle Ed said, "Damn, I am ready for one of those fried pies I saw on the table. Betty, please come in and fix me a pie and some of that homemade ice cream we made last week."

Once the coast was clear, I shared my findings with everyone on the porch. "Please be careful. I don't know what Charles will do next. Just keep an eye on Aunt Betty, and please don't share what I told you. It would break her heart."

"Now that is a damn shame. Baby, don't worry. We will be on the lookout, and we wouldn't dare share this with his mother," Granny said.

Big Mama followed up with, "Little bastard, he ain't what the monkey left on the show ground—other words, he ain't shit."

The whole porch broke out into laugher. "Big Mama cussing, Granny talking trash . . . y'all are good," I said. "I'm going home tomorrow. Until then, I'm going to have pie and ice cream with Uncle Ed and Aunt Betty." When I pulled on the old screen door, my love came down. I turned around and said, "Damn, I love all of you. Thanks so much for all that you do and what you have done."

CHAPTER 13

UP EARLY

Michael

The smell of coffee brewing woke me up. On my way to the bathroom, I could hear Darren moving around in the kitchen. *What is he up to? He's never up this early.*

I walked quietly down the hall to the kitchen, I could hear him on the phone. Not sure who he was talking to, I heard him say, "Don't worry. I'll work it out."

When I walked into the kitchen, he quickly ended the call. With his back to me, he said, "Morning, baby. I didn't mean to wake you up."

Trying not to act suspicious, I replied, "Hi, baby. You're up early."

Instead of responding, he offered to fix me a cup of coffee. Placing the cup on the counter, he said, "Do you remember I told you last month about the five-day conference down in St. Simons Island?"

With my coffee cup close to my lips, I said, "Yes, that conference in South Georgia we're attending together. I'm excited about our little getaway."

Looking disappointed, he said, "I hate to disappoint you—but due to space limitations, we won't be able to bring guests."

Lost for words, I just looked at him for a second with hatred in my heart. I knew damn well he was lying. Instead of responding, I got up and made a bowl of cereal. Then, all I could say was, "Wow, what a shame. I was looking forward to the trip."

On his way out of the kitchen, he said, "Maybe we can go down before the end of the summer. The relaxed setting would help with our family planning."

Without emotions, I replied, "I think that would be a great idea. I'm so sorry you have to attend the conference alone."

When Darren left the room, my phone rang. Looking at the contact, I saw that it was Winston, the godson of Darren's grandmother Rosie, his father's mom.

Eagerly answering, I said, "Well, good morning!"

With that sweet, deep, sexy Jamaican accent, Winston replied, "Good morning, sunshine. I see you are up early. I wanted to let you know I'll be in town late Thursday and was hoping we could connect."

I replied, "Of course, we can connect. Better yet, I would love for you to stay at the house."

"Are you sure?" He hesitated. "The last time I was in town, Darren was a little cold."

Fed up with Darren's lying ass, I said, "I insist. Darren seems to be in a good mood lately, and matter of fact, he'll be out of town. I would love to have your company."

"Well, look for me after seven Thursday night."

Just as I put my phone down, Darren came back and picked up his phone.

"Baby, don't feel bad about the last-minute changes to

your trip. I understand. Business before pleasure," I said before he left again.

With this shit-eating smile, he said, "Baby, thanks for understanding."

"Ya, mon," I blew him a kiss and thought, *Trick-ass liar.*

CHAPTER 14

SHE IS OUT OF TOWN

Joy

I knew I looked like a damn fool standing in the middle of the den, trying to recall the last time I used my phone, it started to ring, which led me to the recliner by the window. Pulling the seat out, my phone fell to the floor.

I picked it up and saw the call was from Michael. I checked her message before calling her back: "Hi, Joy, I'm in line at the gate into the park. Let's hook up at the Grist Mill. No need to call back. See you when you get here. Love you."

I had invited Michael to walk around Stone Mountain Park with me. With Gypsy being out of town, I thought it would be good for us to catch up. Lately, I had been a little hard on her about that "boy of a husband," but she knew I meant well. *At least, I think so, but I don't give a rat's patootie if she doesn't.*

Just as I figured, the line into the park was five cars deep. *They should have a special lane for folk with passes!*

Finally inside, I saw Michael's car, but I didn't see her. When I got out of the car, I heard, "Hi, sis."

Michael was standing behind my car. "What up, sis?" I replied, reaching out for a hug.

Looking down at my sneaker sandals, Michael said, "Are you going to walk in those?"

"Damn real," I said nonchalantly. "I'm going to walk in my sandals. These are on my feet, and they're my shoes. So what? If I was not afraid of stepping in dog shit, I would walk barefoot."

Shaking her head, she said, "Your country butt... let's go."

"All jokes aside, what's wrong with my sandals? They're walking shoes, so what is it?"

Michael replied, "Do you see anyone else wearing them? Those sandals are not in style and never were."

"No, my focus isn't other people's feet. My focus is enjoying our time together. Baby girl, living or dressing in style is a form of mind control. Wall Street does not call it style, they call it profit, just like slavery. Keep in mind slavery was about economics. Real talk, I'm not afraid to dress in my style. Society can take it or leave it alone. I'm a creative free thinker." With my arms around, her, I whispered, "Like my daddy used to tell me, 'Baby, let me put your boots on.'"

Michael asked, "What the *hell* does that mean?"

"It means I'm sharing what I know, not what I heard. Baby girl, you really need to stop worrying about what people think. Learn to play in your sandbox. Make and break your own rules. Again, like my daddy would say, 'Baby, fuck them all' —BFTA. Live *your* damn life."

"I love your daddy's wisdom," Michael laughed.

With pride, I said, "Yes, he was full of raw, uncut wisdom and would tell it like it is. Not only did I hear him, but I also listened. Don't get me wrong. My daddy was sweet, loving, and an awesome provider, but he showed tough love when it came to standing up for yourself and living your life." My voice broke. "Damn, I miss my daddy."

With a gentle rub on my back, Michael said, "So, there is a soft part of you. Never seen it before."

Wiping my eyes, I said, "Yes, there is. I bleed, too, but you just have to cut real deep to make it run."

"Well, you really learned your daddy's lessons. I admire how you stood your ground when my 'fake friends,' as you call them, tried to call you out about how many times you've been married," Michael said.

"Damn real, I stand my ground. Look, baby girl, relationships—whether family, church, emotional, spiritual, business, or friends—are mile markers. Life is a journey, and I navigate through life using an old, tried, trusted, forever-knowing GPS—God's planned signs. You see, I know this GPS will always work. It doesn't have to be charged, rebooted, or recalled. I know it won't send me to the wrong location, and I can trust I'll always arrive at my next destination at the right time, not a second too early or too late.

"I tell you the truth, there is nothing I could do that would prevent me from using this tool, and I know it is forever there for me. But what I have learned is, I can lean on Him for a stress-free journey, and He'll never leave me."

With a look of intrigue, Michael asked, "So, what lessons have you learned on your journey?"

She's actually listening to me and not just hearing me, I thought. "I've learned many, but I have my top five that resonate with me. First and foremost, be thankful for the chariot that God has blessed you with."

With a puzzled look, Michael said, "Chariot?"

"Yes, chariot, a vehicle made for one person—our lovely bodies. That's why I'm so hard on people when they try to remodel their bodies, like something was wrong with God's design. 'Though your butt may not be big as a Caddy, dammit, be thankful for what you got.'

"Second, always greet all of God's creations with a loving smile and pure heart. Make your intentions honest, say what you mean, and mean what you say.

"Third, there will be detours, sunny days, and rainy days. And sometimes there will be storms that'll cause you to just pull over, turn on your caution lights, and ride it out—but the destination never changes.

"Fourth, there will be rest stops along the way where you can relax, grab some food for your soul, fill your tank with good loving, and have a chance to relieve yourself of bad energy. Remember not to rest too long, consume only foods that will not tire you out, and remember your tank holds an infinite amount of love. Take all you need. And for God's sake, when you relieve yourself, do not just sit over it, flush it! Don't look back, wash your hands, and keep it moving. Give forty-five minutes of life to get over fuckery.

"Fifth, stay in your lane and read the signs. Be blessed where you are. Your journey is better for you when it has a price."

Michael shook her head. "It isn't that easy."

"It is, Michael. I always said the way I've been rolling, someday it will all come crashing down. So, every time I start feeling that funny kind of way, the first thing I ask is, 'Lord, is this the day?' No matter how many times I come to this juncture, my angel whispers in my ear, 'Shut down your monkey mind and keep it moving.'

"The bottom line is, God wants us to be happy. He does not want us to live in fear of anything or anyone, and He wants us to concern ourselves with what He wants, not what humans want." Holding Michael's hand, I finished up with, "All of your blessings are standing behind your fears. Just step to the side and let fear pass. Let it get the hell on."

"Michael, let me sum this up. I don't give a rat's ass what people think of me. This is my life, my journey, and my relationship with God. BFTA..."

Squeezing my hand, Michael asked, "You could teach life lessons to the world. Have you ever thought about writing a book?"

I said, "My story is so crazy, it would read like a sci-fi. Anyway, people are so busy judging me, they don't listen. Hell, I doubt they'd read what I have to say. Then again, I bet some would read but deny it. Cowards. How about I write about their jacked-up lives? Now, that would be a sad and scary read."

Michael replied, "Your first book should be about my sad, fake-ass life."

After our walk, Michael opened her car trunk and brought out this beautiful basket full of everything we didn't need to eat.

Dancing around, I said, "Damn, girl, you know how to make good memories. Hey, let's eat under the bridge by the Grist Mill."

Settling down on the rocks, I pulled out my pipe. While packing it with some weed I had in my bra, Michael told me how much she appreciated sharing my experience. Then she followed up with, "Joy, Darren is pressuring me to get pregnant. Girl, it is like he is obsessed. To be honest, I really think he wants a baby to make his family happy. He gives less than a damn about starting a family."

"There's something fishy about the motivation for your 'marriage.' I can't figure it out, but I will. Just because a mofo 'put a ring on it' don't mean cat shit. So superficial. I wish ladies would stop believing that bullshit pop culture illusion and realize Wall Street is using it to brainwash the masses. For me, fuck the ring. I need a mofo to but his crown on my head. Are you following me?"

Michael answered, "Not really."

"Baby, let me explain. Listen to what I'm saying. When a man gives you his crown, you are his queen, the most powerful chess piece on the game called life. She moves unobstructed. She reigns over his kingdom. He seeks and trusts her wisdom. When a man loves his queen, he can't hold another girl.

"Now, a wife is a person who signed a contract called 'marriage.' She only has the power of a wife. They exchange scripted vows. All expected of him is to say, 'I do,' and put a ring on it. To be honest, I never attended a wedding where a man committed to his queen—including mine. When a king and queen combine their light, one does not make the other dimmer. Together they shine a blinding light over their kingdom.

"Another thing, when you are a queen, you don't have to think like a man. You are his queen. He wants you to act and think as his queen—poised, polished, and confident. A real man wants his queen to stay focused on their kingdom. Shit, if you must think like a man to deal with your king, then you need to leave and let him be with a man."

What I shared must have resonated, because Michael closed her eyes and sat in silence before replying, "Damn, never thought about it like that."

Hugging her, I whispered, "Now you know. Baby, I am sharing what my daddy taught me and what a long-lost lover gave me."

Looking straight ahead, Michael asked, "Can I share a secret?"

Puzzled—because why would she ask for permission to tell me a secret?—I said, "Hell yeah. Start talking."

She took a couple of hits off the pipe and got to it. "Darren and his mama have been pressuring me to have a baby, and to be honest I don't want to look at any of his demons, so guess what I did?"

"I can't guess, but if it were me, I would cut his dick off, cook it up in some cabbage, and feed it to him and his mean-ass mama."

When I said that, Michael fell back, threw her legs up in the air, and screamed, "I asked for that response!" Sitting back up, she said, "Well, last week, I got an IUD. Girl, he thinks something is wrong with one of us. When he is humping—which isn't often—I want to whisper in his ear, 'It's not you, baby.'"

With my mouth wide open, I screamed, "You cute little fox!"

Looking up at the sunny sky, Michael shared, "Darren will be out later this week. If Gypsy is back in town, let's have a pajama party. Invite Gus. Darren will leave on Thursday and will be gone until Monday. Let's start the party on Friday. Hell, we can party all weekend."

Like a proud mama, I said, "Damn, baby girl, I think I'm rubbing off on you."

With a cute smile, Michal said, "By the way, Winston, Rosie's godson, called to let me know he'll be in town on Thursday. Being family, I invited him to stay at the house."

"Wait, Michael, help me understand. Winston is Rosie's godson, so he's Darren's godbrother?"

"I guess. Darren hates him, but I like him."

"You *naughty* little fox. So, let me ask—what kind of invitation are you offering him?"

With her head to the side, Michael replied, "You know, Darren thinks I'm so dumb. Girl, he had the nerve to say he taught me everything I know. When he said that, I thought, 'No, baby, you taught me everything *you* know."

"Wait. Forget Darren and his bullshit. Are you going to let Winston take care of that thang?"

"I might."

Lost for words, I hugged her around the neck. All I could say was, "Damn, Michael, karma is a mofo. I love it, love you, love it all."

Michael screamed, "Damn real. BFTA!"

CHAPTER 15

WHO DOES THAT?

Joy

Damn. I had every closet packed, coats, formal and informal dresses, shoes, boots—and in different sizes. My goal was to donate anything I hadn't worn in the last year to the shelter for homeless ladies. Hoarding is selfish. *These clothes need to be hanging on the back of a less fortunate queen.*

In the middle of my purge, TJ and Maxx barked. Checking the security cameras, I saw Gypsy getting out of her car. Being out this late wasn't normal for her, and by the way she was walking, I could tell something was up.

Soon as I opened the door, she rushed in. "Hey, I need a drink." Before I closed the door, I peeked out to make sure no one was behind her.

When I got to the kitchen, she was sitting with her head on the counter.

Curious, I asked, "Girl, what the hell is wrong with you?"

"It is my Aunt Betty," she sobbed.

Confused, I said, "Wait. I thought you took care of her last month."

Pushing the barstool back, she said, "I thought so, too, but things have gone from sad to madness."

Lost for words, all I could do was serve up several shots of whiskey and fire up my peace pipe.

After she calmed down, she went into the details of her horror. "Charles, my Aunt Betty's low-down son, slid down to the farm to 'spend time with his mom.' Joy, to be honest, I'm not surprised. I knew he was going to show up once he realized all his mom's accounts were locked, but I didn't think he'd take it this far. After breakfast, everyone thought he and his mom were sitting on the porch, until my cousin Austin, who is a probate judge, called to check on Aunt Betty."

Puzzled, I asked, "Why?"

"See, Charles showed up at the courthouse inquiring about Aunt Betty's property. Feeling like something wasn't right, the clerk notified Austin. When Austin came out, Charles looked like a scared cat and said he was moving his mom to Atlanta and wanted to help her organize her estate before leaving. Surprised, Austin said he would stop by the farm for dinner so they could catch up. He meandered around the counter until Charles received the tax records. Austin said when Charles read through the records, you could see steam coming out of his nose. Charles showed Austin the tax records and shouted, 'Hell, no! What is this?' Charles asked.

"In that dry, matter-of-fact way of his, Austin replied, 'Wow, I didn't realize Gypsy had so much property.'

"Spitting fire, Charles claimed it had to be a mistake. To calm him down, Austin promised to look over the papers when they hooked up at the farm. Noticing Aunt Betty was uncomfortable, he suggested taking his mom back to the farm."

I asked, "So why did Austin call if they were going back to the farm?"

"Joy, from my understanding, Austin noticed when Charles pulled out of the parking lot, he went in the opposite direction of the farm. So, he called Big Mama, and Big Mama called the sheriff. Sheriff Hunter told her he ran into Charles at the gas station, and Charles told him they were heading to Fernandina Beach, Florida. Charles and Aunt Betty never showed up at the farm, and later that night Big Mama got a call from some homeless shelter in Jacksonville, Florida, asking about Aunt Betty."

I jumped straight up in disbelief. "How in the hell did she end up in a homeless shelter?"

Voice shaking, Gypsy said, "Once Charles realized that he nor his mom had no access to her major bank accounts, he just dropped her off at the door of the shelter and hauled ass. We were told she stood on the curb all day. When someone checked on her, she gave them her emergency contact card that was in her purse. Then she just walked away. When my family was contacted, they called the sheriff, then they called me."

Handing her another shot, I asked, "So, what's your plan?"

With her head back, Gyspy replied, "My car is packed, and I'm heading out when I leave here."

Knowing she was not in any shape to drive to the mailbox, let alone drive to Waycross, I told her I would drive her. When I said that, she looked at me and said, "Girl, you are just as high as I am." Standing up from the bar, Gypsy suggested we lie down on the sofa to try to sober up.

While we lounged on the sofa, Gus called. When I answered, he asked, "Is everything okay? You sound stressed."

I shared with him what was going on. "I'm about to call

Michael to come get TJ and Maxx so we can get on the road. Our plan was to leave an hour back, but we are too upset to drive."

When I said that, Gypsy looked at me and just rolled off the sofa.

There was a long pause on the phone, then Gus said, "I don't think you both should be on the road at this time of night, and you sound really upset. I'll drive you all down. You have the keys to Roc's RV, and I'm sure he wouldn't mind. No need to have Michael pick the dogs up. The dogs can help me watch out for the highway patrol. Leave the key in your mailbox. I'll go pick up the RV from the storage park."

I texted Roc the plan and he replied, NO WORRIES. DRIVE SAFE. Later another text from Roc popped up: SO DOES THIS GET ME OFF THE HOOK FOR THE CAMPING TRIP?

I quickly texted, NO.

I told Gypsy to make some coffee—we needed to sober up—and to call Michael. While packing, I saw the RV park in front of the house.

When Gus came in, he said, "Look, ladies, I got you all covered. Remember, God is in control, and he'll guide our steps right straight to Aunt Betty's smiling face."

To our surprise, Michael stopped by with a huge love basket. Being her sweet self, she even packed TJ and Maxx their own basket. While we packed, she set up the RV for travel with clean towels, sheets, and bathroom amenities. She even stocked the fridge.

Before leaving, Gus led us in prayer. "God please keep us safe and guide our steps, Amen."

After the prayer, TJ and Maxx jumped in the copilot seat and we headed out.

CHAPTER 16

LORD, SHOW ME THE PATH

Gypsy

When Gus turned onto the road to the farm, my emotions went from contempt for Charles to the love for my family and my friends. I guess my family saw our headlights, because as soon as we turned into the drive, the front porch light came on. When we reached the top of the drive, I stood up and said, "Thank you, God, for a safe trip. Friends, welcome to the farm."

After saying, "Amen," Joy said, "Bet Big Mama will be up early making her famous blueberry pancakes."

After parking, Gus took the dogs for a quick walk. I started to gather my things. "Joy, I should crash with you all tonight, but I know my grandparents will not go to sleep until I walk into the house—and to be honest, I'm feeling a little blue. I'm sure sleeping in Aunt Betty's bed would make me feel a little better."

Reaching out for a hug, Joy said, "Baby, I understand. Tell everyone I will see them in the morning."

With a smile, I replied, "You know they're looking forward to seeing you."

Just as I opened the RV door, Big Daddy was standing there, smiling from ear to ear. When Joy heard his voice, she came out. Reaching for both of us, he said, "It is so good to see my girls." Looking at the open RV door, he asked, "Where are TJ and Maxx?"

Joy replied, "Don't worry. We wouldn't leave home without them. Our friend Gus is taking them for a walk."

The sounds of the farm—rooster crows, chatter, and the slamming of the kitchen screen door—made me smile. Sitting up, I realized not only did I fall asleep on top of the handmade quilt Big Mama made last year, but I was also still dressed from last night.

Before walking to the shower, I fell on my knees and asked God, "Please show me the path to take. Keep Aunt Betty safe and keep me out of my emotions. With the blood of Jesus, amen."

When I stood up, my attention went to Aunt Betty's Bible. It was open at Joshua 1, highlighted: "Have I not commanded you? Be strong and courageous. Do not be afraid; do not be discouraged, for the LORD your God will be with you wherever you go."

After I took my shower, for some strange reason, I felt the need to wear something of Aunt Betty's, so I grabbed a cute sundress and some matching sandals she had tucked away in her closet.

After getting dressed, I stood in the mirror and whispered, "Auntie, I am coming to get you. I pray that your shoes lead me straight to you. Just hold on. Now, let's do what I do best when I'm on the farm—eat."

When I got to the kitchen, Big Mama was standing at the stove making her famous blueberry pancakes. Waiting until the last cake was turned, I said, "Hey, pretty lady."

Quickly turning quickly around, she did a happy dance toward me. Reaching for a hug, all she said was, "Thank you, Lord."

While the cakes were cooking, I stood at the kitchen window watching TJ and Maxx running around the fenced-in backyard. I pulled Big Mama to the window. "Girl, look at them."

With her arms around my waist, she said, "Child, they been out there all morning. They need to be running around. Both just finished a big bowl of chicken and rice."

"So, where is everybody?"

With her hands on her shapely hips, Big Mama said, "Well, your granny went out to the shed for a bottle of homemade cane syrup, and your Big Daddy is rounding up everyone for breakfast."

Just as Big Mama finished all the pancakes, Granny came in with two bottles of syrup. Setting one on the table, she handed the other bottle to me and said, "Take this one home."

The three of us sat at the table sipping on hot cups of coffee. Looking at the two of them, it still amazed me how identical they are.

Before we finished our second cup, the kitchen was packed with Gus, Joy, and all my aunts and uncles. When Joy noticed the blueberry pancakes, she ran over and gave Big Mama a hug. Looking over at me, she mouthed, "I told you."

After Big Daddy blessed the food, he told everyone, "We should have one leader of Aunt Betty's search team, and I think it should be Gypsy. Do we all agree?"

Without hesitation, everyone agreed.

Honored, I accepted the responsibility. "Thanks for trusting me. Let's talk strategy after we enjoy this lovely breakfast."

After breakfast, I asked everyone to come back to the table so I could share my thoughts on finding our Aunt Betty. I opened the family meeting by reading the highlighted text from Aunt Betty's Bible. Then I read the message from Sheriff Hunter saying Charles was last seen about thirty miles outside of Jacksonville. Unfortunately, he was alone. He contacted the sheriff in Jacksonville, and a silver alert had been activated.

"So, family, I am going to leave law enforcement to the police. The sheriff has promised to keep in contact with the Jacksonville police and will text me any updates. Next, my friends and I are going to check out all of the homeless shelters in the area." Looking at the concerned faces, I asked, "Are you all comfortable with this approach?"

After everyone agreed, I followed up with, "Please continue to look around town, and keep your phones close by. Send me any updates that you come across." Trying to put on a happy face, I ended our meeting with, "Let's bring our family back home. Be safe, and I love you all."

When everyone left, Big Daddy handed me the keys to Aunt Betty's car. "Baby, use her car. I just had it serviced last week, and the gas tank is full."

"Please keep an eye on Maxx. He will run away if he gets half the chance," Joy said to Big Daddy.

"Don't worry. I'm getting ready to give both a bath. They'll be in the house for the rest of the day."

I gave Gus the keys, I said, "Well, we are back on the road."

At the end of the drive, Gus stopped and asked, "Make a right or left?"

I replied, "Knowing Charles has been in town, I think

we should stop by Aunt Betty's house on our way to Jacksonville."

Gus and Joy replied at the same time, "Good idea."

I told Gus to turn left, then I put my aunt's address into his GPS and we sat quietly listening to the directions.

When we reached my aunt's house, I told Gus to park close to the front door. Once inside, it was obvious Charles had been there. All the TVs and appliances were missing.

With a look of shock, Gus said, "Why would he steal his mother's refrigerator and the damn stove?"

When Gus asked me that, my heart dropped suddenly. I ran into the living room and fell to my knees. With my butt in the air and practically under the sofa, I screamed, "Thank God I listened to my spirit voice when it told me to hide my aunt's antique tea set!"

While sitting on the floor next to the sofa, I called Big Daddy. "I stopped by Aunt Betty's house to check on the house. Looks like Charles has been here."

"Please tell me he did not take his mom's tea set."

Exhaling, I replied, "Thank God, I hid it under the sofa. Can you come pick it up?"

After I hung up with Big Daddy, Joy and Gus came in and sat on the sofa. Joy asked, "Why are you so emotional about this tea set?"

"Y'all, this is not just any tea set. This set has American history."

With a puzzled look, Gus asked, "What the hell are you talking about? Was it used in the Boston Tea Party?"

"Big Mama's great-grandmother hid it during the Civil War, and it has been in the family ever since," I shared.

Amazed, Gus said, "I am glad you told your Big Daddy to come pick it up. God forbid Charles finds it and sells it in some dingy crack house."

Disgusted, Joy said, "Look how he trashed his mom's house. This is so sad. What happened to him?"

"As a child, Charles was so smart and sweet, he loved fishing, and was a big help to his mom. We noticed the change in him after he came home from Chicago. His mom put him in rehab, but I guess he still needs help. My take is, once you consume the devil's sperm, he owns you."

Joy replied, "Like my daddy used to say, 'You never know what you are feeding.'"

While looking at his phone, Gus said, "I see there's a hardware store a couple of blocks from here. I'm going to pick up a couple of locks and nails to secure the house."

After Gus left, Joy and I started to throw out all the food in the kitchen pantry. On my way to the trash, I heard someone walking around the house. Whispering, I asked Joy, "Did you hear that?"

With a knife from the open drawer, Joy replied, "Yep, I think I hear someone walking under the window."

When we saw them try to push the window next to the kitchen up, we fell to the floor and crawled out of the kitchen. Trying not to be heard, Joy whispered in my ear, "We need to call the police. Where's your phone?"

Shaking, I said, "Damn, I left my phone on the sofa."

"Look, don't stand up. Let's just crawl to the sofa."

Before we reached the sofa, we heard footsteps on the porch. I asked Joy, "Do you think it's Gus?"

Motioning for me to crawl back into the kitchen, Joy replied, "No, he has on sneakers. The footsteps sound like someone has on hard-bottom shoes."

Before we made it to the kitchen, we heard the door open. We were so scared that we froze and just started screaming. When we looked up, Gus and Big Daddy were standing at the door. "What in the hell are you two doing?" Big Daddy shouted.

Looking up, I told them, "Joy and I heard someone trying to push up the window. We assumed it was a burglar."

Big Daddy said, "Ladies, I'm sorry. I was checking the windows. I didn't see the car, so I thought you all had left."

Gus asked Joy, "What were you going to do with that knife, stab them in the foot?"

All of us laughed so hard until we cried.

With his hand over his heart, Big Daddy said, "It is good to hear laughter again in this old house."

While Gus changed the locks, Joy and I went back into the kitchen. This time, I had my phone.

Big Daddy came into the kitchen and said, "It would break your aunt's heart if she saw this mess."

I agreed, "It would have killed her if he stole the tea set."

After changing the locks, Gus came into the kitchen and said, "It's getting late. We need to get on the road."

Big Daddy got up, boxed up the tea set, and took it to his truck. Just as Big Daddy came back in, the sheriff called. I answered with the speaker on.

Excited, Sheriff Hunter said, "Aunt Betty was dropped off at the hospital here in town. Meet me there. One more thing—please bring some clean clothes and a pair of shoes for her."

Concerned about the family, I told Big Daddy, "Please go back to the farm. I'll call you when I get to the hospital."

"I think that's a good idea."

Gus turned to Big Daddy and said, "I don't feel comfortable with you driving alone. I'm going to drive you home. Joy and Gypsy can handle things at the hospital."

When we reached the hospital, the doctor was still evaluating Aunt Betty, who became very emotional when she saw us. It broke my heart to see her scared and crying. After her evaluation, the doctor told us she was fine, just a little dehydrated.

I asked Joy to stay with Aunt Betty while I spoke to the doctor. In the middle of the update, Sheriff Hunter walked up. Looking at the sheriff, the doctor said, "Perfect timing. Ms. Betty has bruises on her back and neck. Obviously, they are not self-inflicted, and they don't look like she had an accident. I'm going to have the nurse take pictures, and I am filing an elder-abuse report."

After the update, the sheriff told the doctor, "As of now, this is an active investigation. I will send someone over to secure her clothes and to take pictures."

Still visibly upset, the doctor said, "Will do. I think someone has some explaining to do."

When the doctor walked away, Sheriff Hunter told me, "Larry, a local trucker that was helping with the search, found Aunt Betty barefoot and confused, wandering around a truck stop outside of town. He called me to let me know she was with him, and he was on his way home. I had an ambulance meet them on the highway, and they took her to the hospital." With a hurt look, he said, "Gypsy, get this. The only way he was able to get her in his truck was to promise to take her and Charles to the beach."

After he finished, I asked, "So, that's why you asked me to bring the clothes and shoes?"

"Yes. I am keeping all of her clothes as evidence, but to be honest, you know I've known your family all my life, spent my summers fishing with Charles, and I was not going to let her leave the hospital, dirty, and barefoot."

With a soft rub on his back, I said, "Thank you for your hard work and for just caring."

After we wrapped things up, he asked, "Is it okay for me to speak with Aunt Betty? I just want to let her know I didn't forget about her."

With tears, I replied, "I think that would be a great idea."

After seeing Aunt Betty, the sheriff told me he was on his way to the farm and he would leave it to me to give all the details to the family.

Before leaving, Sheriff Hunter stopped and said, "I grew up with Charles. I know how good his mom's been to him, and to see this madness pisses me off. Trust me, I am going to do all I can to bring him in."

After the police finished their report, Joy and I helped Aunt Betty dress. For a moment, I didn't care if she was fragile, bruised, and dehydrated; all that mattered to me was that I was able to take her back to our family alive.

CHAPTER 17

PLAYAS' SECRETS REVEALED

Joy

After we returned from rescuing Aunt Betty, I stopped by Michael's to see what she was up to. When I got there, she and Gypsy were sitting in the kitchen.

Gypsy looked up and said, "Damn, girl, we are thinking alike. Now that could be dangerous."

"That could be a little scary." With a hug, I said, "Michael, thanks, baby girl, for all that you do."

Michael replied, "My pleasure. You ladies are my big sisters." Placing a plate of cookies on the counter, Michael said, "It's Friday night. Ladies, let the good times roll."

Still concerned, I asked Gypsy, "How is Aunt Betty, and how are you doing?"

"Aunt Betty is fine, and I'm good." Then she followed up with, "Ladies, tonight, I don't want to think about anything but what we're doing at this moment."

Michael replied, "Baby, I understand." Looking over at

me, Michael asked, "So, Joy, how are things going with you and Gus? You all did hang out in the RV for a couple of days. So, what's up?"

Jumping up, I replied, "Now that you asked, let me tell you. I finally figured out why Gus and I never connected."

Gypsy placed her drink down and said, "What the hell?"

"Ladies, hear me out. I remembered the last time we went on a trip together. I tell no lie, sixty percent of the time he talked about his mother, thirty percent of the time he talked to her on the phone, and ten percent of the time he talked to me. That's why I took him out of rotation the first time. He is a son-husband."

"I am afraid to ask, but what the hell is a son-husband?" Gypsy asked warily.

"Let me explain. I figured this out when I was with Mess Number Two. Remember how I shared with you how he was with this woman for over fifteen years and never married her? His mama stayed with them off and on—more on than off—for the entire time. As we grew closer, I asked questions about his family relationships. Based on what he shared, I coined the name son-husband."

With her hand on her hips, Michael shouted, "Girl, in the south, we call them mama's boys."

"No, no, I am not talking about a mama's boy. I view a mama's boy as a son who is very sensitive to his mama's needs. He shows his appreciation of her struggles. Now, a son-husband is created by some lonely mama that tries to capture her man's love vicariously through her son."

Gypsy said, "And that's different from a mama's boy, how?"

"Okay, ladies, strap up. Let me take you there. The mama's old man makes her feel second best. He might have even brought home a baby or two. She knows what she is working with, but she loves him, so she stays but never makes it to queen status. She doesn't realize if you tolerate this type of situation, then you were never his queen.

"I call this type of woman a wife-mama. In her altered state of reality, she clings to her only son as if he is her old man's mini-him. He is the shadow of her old man; her wants will shape him into what she wants her old man to be. The son is under her control. She will domesticate him, lean on him for emotional support, companionship, and he'll be her knight in shining armor, a safe place where she can love. Intimacy, not an issue. She has her memories. When her old man finally leaves her sad, lonely, tortured life, she is so scared to be hurt again. So, for whatever reason, she promotes mini-him to son-husband status.

"He wants for nothing. He will dress better, ride better, everything better than his siblings, and will get away with whatever. He is the man of the house, and he will have the last word. The siblings rationalize the situation by saying Mom and her son have this 'special relationship.' But deep in their hurt, they hate him. This hurt will raise its ugly head when wife-mama becomes disabled or dies.

"When it's time for him to leave home, she'll make him feel guilty. If he moves far away, where she can't see him every day, the money stops, but once he's closer and back under her control, he will be well taken care of. New car, best of clothes, control of her home and finances.

"One more thing: if there's an uncle, brother, or best friend around, they will make sure the daddy's legacy continues. Birds of a feather will flock together. Knowing the husband's true nature, they'll secretly teach him all the tricks wife-mama hated—'the hoe-dog game.' See, wife-mama will not live forever. So, between wife-mama and his mentors, he is at the crossroads called the four Ps."

Standing at full attention, Michael and Gypsy screamed, "What the hell are the four Ps?"

Looking at both, I said, "He will be a pimp, player, politician, or a preacher."

Arms raised above her head, Gypsy said, "I know I shouldn't ask you to explain, but I'm dumb enough to ask."

"Not a dumb question," I said. "All of them play from the same playbook—paper chasing, taking minds hostage. The only difference is the window dressing. They've learned how to say a lot that means nothing but draws in the marginalized. Do you remember Jim Jones? He reached out to all these people and played on their vulnerability. These son-husbands do the same thing. They learned mind control from the cradle. Now that wife-mama has him all pimped out, his mentors, his uncles, or whoever are going to show him how to build out his stable, and most of all, how to get paid and how to get taken care of.

"As the son-husband gets older, he'll follow his mentors' advice and find a woman with low self-esteem, just like his dad. The ones that will be so glad to have a good-looking, smooth player. Back to Mess Number Two, do you all remember him?"

Michael said, "We all remember that fine piece of work."

"He was drop-dead gorgeous, but I was not impressed. Why? Because my daddy made him look like a clown. See, I'm used to real smooth, pretty men. So, Mess Number Two had this victim—not attractive, adopted, didn't have a solid family foundation. Mess Number Two never talked about this woman, even though they were together for fifteen years and she helped take care of his mama. His family acted like she never walked this earth. I just had to know how in the hell he got away with that.

"She had four children, but she had a good job, paid enough for Mama, and by this time, Mama's funds were running low. First, he made her feel like she was a part of the family—in family photos, babysitting, family trips, entertained, etc. He would give her tokens to keep her hope alive.

"So, wife-mama moved in with them, would be up in the morning when this poor woman left for work and would be there when she got home. This woman cooked and cleaned for her, even though she was working. Why? Because that is what a wife does. She forgot she was not the wife; she was a victim. How could he marry her? He had a wife, his wife-mama.

"Before I move on, let me make this clear—never play wife. If he wants you to act like a wife, he'll make you a wife. If it doesn't work out, get a divorce."

Looking like she figured out a cure for cancer, Gypsy shouted, "So, that is why you've been married so many times."

Clapping, I said, "Damn real. Shit, my daddy didn't raise a trick. He made sure I knew the game. Me personally, I don't spend a lot of time practicing marriage. If you're serious, invest your time. If it doesn't work out, cash out. Ladies, wait. I am in no ways finished.

"So, Mama told her son-husband not to marry her. She was too old, and she didn't fit in—meaning she was too ugly to show off to her friends—and she had kids.

"You see, Mama was a user just like he was. Remember,

she made him. She controlled him. They were the same. Remember, shit does not fall far from the ass. It was okay for him to play house—it was comfortable for Mama—but he couldn't marry her. It was not about financial gain. It was about keeping Mama. I call it free assisted living.

"Not only was son-husband playing her, but so were the siblings. They did not have the same bond with Mama and really did not want to be bothered with her when Mama got sick. So, when Mama decided to go back home for good, Mess Number Two went back home with Mama to 'take care of her,' but they were done using up that victim's love, finances, and home. When Mama was about to die, here comes the siblings. They took Mama straight to the cleaners—money, property, furs, and jewelry. Son-husband cried foul. 'Why are you not helping me take care of Mama?' he said.

"See, he didn't realize he has being used by his wife-mama. The siblings' attitude was, 'She was never here for us, it was all about you, so you need to be all about her.' Once the mother was old and fragile, the son-husband cooked, cleaned, washed, bathed her, changed her diapers, and wore himself out. His siblings were like, 'Put her in a home,' but he stayed there to the end. In the end, he realized what he had given up—family, a wife, genuine love. Then his loving eyes started to understand he, too, was a victim.

"Then one day, here comes me. Early on, he tried to play this mind game with me, but my dad taught me better. Then Mama meets me. I'm what she wanted for her family. I fit in, like I freaking cared. Funny, I had to let them know early on the neck of the woods I'm from. I'm loved, and I didn't need his dysfunctional family. I refused to be one of his victims. Their karma was me. I let him know upfront, 'Your mama is not living with us. I am not taking care of her. She has daughters. Let them do it.' Occasionally, she would get 'sick' and expect him to run home, and when he got there, she was, let's just say, much better."

Gypsy asked, "So, why did you divorce?"

"I tell you why. He broke the rule."

"What rule?"

"If I cannot be your queen, then I need to move on. So, that's what I did."

Putting her drink down, Michael asked, "So, what does that have to do with Gus?"

"Well, my theory is if it quacks like a duck and walks like a duck, you don't call it a goat. Gus was a son-husband. Once I figured that out, I moved on. At the time I didn't know what to call it, but I wasn't comfortable. I'm going to Jacksonville with him next week. Maybe he can work his way back on the team. If not, he will always be my friend. We just won't be getting naked."

Responding, Michael asked, "You are just going to share a room like brother and sister?"

"Girl, no. He agreed to adjoining rooms."

Chiming in, Gypsy asked, "What has changed with Gus? I thought you said son-husbands can't love two women. So, why are you even thinking about it?"

"Just like a marriage, the vow is, 'Until death do us part.' His mom died last year. He is free to love without feeling like he is cheating on his wife. He was and still is a lovely man, but at that time he wasn't emotionally available. I really think he needs to go to therapy. He might not change, but it can make him aware."

Hand over her mouth, Michael said, "Damn. This makes sense. That's what Darren is—but it was his grandmother Tee, not his mama."

"Same dog, different fleas."

CHAPTER 18

POOR GUS

Joy

Gus and I arrived in Jacksonville late. When we checked in, the lady at the front desk looked puzzled when we asked for adjoining rooms.

Gus left early for work. I slept in until nine a.m.

After a morning swim, I laid around the pool for a couple of hours looking at the *City Magazine* on the table next to my chair. I noticed the mall Michael recommended was on the front cover. Looking through the list of stores, I decided to spend the day checking it out. The day was so pretty; I decided to walk. The travel app on my phone showed it was only three miles from the hotel with a walk time of forty-five minutes.

When I got back to the room, I made sure I set my phone alarm for 4:00 to make sure I got back before 6:00 for dinner with Gus. On my way out, I noticed Gus had left the adjoining door slightly open. Since I was walking, there was no need for me to carry the car keys, so I left the keys with a note in his room.

When I stepped outside of the hotel, it felt like a sauna—hot and wet. Luckily, the hotel shuttle was out front, and the driver was sitting inside. "Excuse me, will you be able to drop me off at the River Walk Mall?" I asked.

The driver, a young man with bleached blond hair and a deep-brown tan, replied, "Sure. Are you ready to leave now?"

When I told him I was, he stood up, introduced himself as Stan, and handed me his contact information. "When you're ready for a pickup, please call the number on the front."

Sitting behind Stan, I told him, "My intention this morning was to walk, but this heat changed my mind quick."

Stan laughed. "I understand. It's easy to get dehydrated in this Florida heat."

When we reached the entrance to the mall, Stan said, "Before getting out, please grab yourself a bottled water from the cooler next to your seat."

I grabbed the water, tipped Stan, and jumped out of the shuttle.

The mall's floor-to-ceiling windows gave me the feeling of being outside. The aroma from the food court made me hungry. As I walked up the stairs, I stopped to watch the pretty glass elevator that was the center point in the mall. Just when I was about to continue my journey, the loving couple getting off the elevator caught my eye. I watched them walk toward the front of the mall. I couldn't see the front of the man's face, but damn, his side profile looked just like Darren.

I guess it's true we all have a twin, but damn.

In a slow jog, I was able to watch the couple from behind.

Not only does he look like Darren, but he also damn sure walks like him . . .

Being me, I took out my phone and started taking pictures, whispering, "Turn around so I can get a good shot." Looking at my pictures, I only got a side view, and it wasn't clear.

When they got to the door, he pulled out his wallet and handed the lady something. Then he left, leaving her in the mall.

When he left, I followed the lady into a high-end shop. *I'm taking a couple shots of her. Never know what I'm seeing or not seeing.* When the lady walked up to the jewelry counter and raised her hand, something about her ring caught my eye. Acting like I was looking at my phone, I was able to get a shot of the ring.

I got close enough to hear her tell the salesperson something about her fiancé. When I heard that, I thought maybe my eyes were playing tricks on me, so I ended my pursuit.

After shopping around for a couple of hours, I left the mall and strolled along the riverfront. Looking around, I realized I was around the corner from the hotel. Hot and hungry, I stopped at this swanky restaurant, the Sea Candy, for a light lunch. The young lady at the door greeted me and said, "Lunch is self-seating."

On my way to a table, I noticed this handsome man with snow-white hair sitting at the bar. I guess I was staring hard, because he smiled. When he smiled, I could see his teeth were as white as his hair. I smiled back, then I scanned the room for a table that gave me a clear view of the man—I mean bar.

The server came over and handed me the menu, then asked if I wanted to order a cocktail.

"Sure. Since I'm not driving, how about a double shot of my favorite whiskey, Uncle Nearest?"

I guess I never lost my taste for good shine—I mean whiskey, I thought.

Waiting on my drink, I looked at the pictures of the couple from the mall, especially the lady's ring. Still not trusting my eyes, I enlarged the hand on the picture, did a screenshot, then enlarged that picture.

Wait, this ring looks just like the ring Michael lost! I could feel my feet bobbing and weaving under the table. I had to calm down. Nobody could be that rotten, not even Darren. Right? My mind told my eyes, *Don't believe what you're seeing.*

To bring myself to a better place, I looked for that thang with the snow-white hair. Scanning the bar, he was nowhere to be found. *Damn. See? Thinking about the wrong things, I missed an opportunity to get a shot of "that purty thang."*

After placing my order, I played a couple of card games until my food arrived.

Suddenly, I felt someone standing behind me. *Is this the man from across the room? Now, that would be a treat.*

Before I could turn around, a familiar hand touched my shoulder. As I thought to myself, *Hell no, it can't be,* the hand moved slowly across my back. When I turned around, all I could say was, "L?"

With the back of his hand, he slowly brushed my face. Looking straight through the back of my eyeballs, he said, "My sweet Candy."

Without warning, a little tear just rolled down my cheeks.

That thick, silky mane, all white, was slicked back, not a strand out of place. His soft-brown skin looked like sun-kissed bronze. His face was baby-smooth except for a perfectly trimmed mustache sitting right over his full lips like a crown, and his unibrow, white but manly shaped. The English, custom-made suit draped over his body with pride. His presence, like always, was magnetic. Every man and woman just had to look. Some just stopped and completely stared, and some peeked. One thing I knew for sure, everybody in the restaurant walked out with the image of him in their imagination.

By the time I pulled myself together, all I could say was, "Why did you walk out of my life? Why? Why?"

Looking at me like he could feel my pain, he replied, "Yes, baby, I owe you so many answers." Pulling out the chair right next to me, he sat down with his arm resting on the back of my chair. When he started to talk to me, my heart broke. "Candy, at the time, your innocence was the light of my dark, evil, cutthroat world. I was living wrong, trying to live right. You were young, sexy, and smart, and I was preoccupied with what-ifs. What if the cops would come in? What if someone had the crazy idea to rob me? What if my enemies found out how weak I was for you?

"When my brother talked about you, my heart ached. I would tell him to leave that little girl alone and stay focused, even though I was just as bad.

"It killed me when you told me you were going away to college. Fighting between what I desired and what was best for you, I surrendered to the latter. But I could not allow you to go to college without being made love to. I knew those college boys were young, dumb, and full of cum. I knew what it was like to make love to a woman. I still have that blood-stained sheet."

I asked, "Why did you stop answering my calls? You just dropped me. I felt like you used me and kicked me aside."

He told me that was so far from the truth. "There were three things I needed to stop: touching you, wanting you, and loving you. I couldn't make a choice, so I walked away saying nothing. But when you left, my life sped up beyond my wildest dreams and nightmares."

I said, "I must tell you, it made me feel so special when you came to my college graduation, and you know you messed me up with your marriage prediction."

"So, Candy, how many times did you marry?"

Embarrassed, I said, "Do I really have to answer?"

L said, "Six. My cousin, your old friend Terri, has been my little spy."

In the middle of our reunion, the alarm on my phone went off. Looking at the alert, I saw ONE HOUR BEFORE DINNER.

Oh, hell. Gus.

I guess L noticed my disappointed expression. Holding my hand, he said, "Baby, I hope everything is okay."

"Yes, I'm okay. I have an appointment in an hour. I need to leave in thirty minutes."

Then the server brought my food, and I told her I needed to leave and to pack it to go.

"Baby, I understand. I have so much more to share with you. I am going to be honest with you. I have your contact information."

Looking surprised, I said, "How in the hell did you get my number? Wait. Let me guess. Terri?"

"I held onto it, hoping one day we would connect."

My heart led me to say, "Please keep in touch. Feel free to call anytime."

Without warning, he kissed me and said, "Thank you."

When the server brought my food, L took the bill. Walking out of the restaurant together, I felt like I did when he gave me my first kiss.

On my way back to the hotel, all I thought about was L. Damn, just like magic, he woke up my love. I just hoped he would do something with it. *If he were the old L, he would do something wonderful with my love. Damn, please tell me that is not Gus standing at the front desk.*

Stan the shuttle driver saw me walk in, greeted me, and asked how the mall was.

When I responded, Gus turned around. Walking up to me, he asked how my day was, then, looking at the bag in my hand, he said, "Tell me you did not go to the Sea Candy for lunch. I wanted to go there for dinner."

I almost dropped the damn bag. Acting like I was disappointed, I replied, "Wow, I'm sorry I spoiled your surprise. Boy, you look like you had a long day."

"Yes, it was, and I'm a little tired."

"What's your routine when you travel?"

Yawning, he said, "Usually, I would eat in my room."

"Well, that is what we are going to do. Keep in mind you're on a business trip. I'm just hanging out. There are several restaurants across the street—Mexican, Chinese, and a deli. I'll pick you up something and we can eat by the pool. Here, take my food upstairs. I'll eat it tomorrow."

In the middle of my madness, the damn phone started to vibrate.

Reaching for my bag, Gus replied, "That's a great idea. The Mexican restaurant across the street caught my eye. Pick me up a couple of chicken tacos."

On my way to the restaurant, I checked my voice message. "Hi, Candy, just checking on you. Text or call when you can. Baby, touching you again, you took me over the moon. Now, don't get married on me. Love you."

After I placed the order, I thought, *I know if I call L, hanging up will be hard for me. Let me play it safe with a simple text.*

HEY, BABY, I AM OVER THE MOON WITH YOU. I SEE YOU

STILL HAVE JOKES. WILL CALL YOU WHEN I GET BACK TO ATLANTA. LOVE YOU.

Before paying for my order, I texted Gus. HI, MEET ME AT THE POOL IN 15 MINS.

When I got back to the hotel, Gus was standing outside. Giving him one of the bags, I said, "Now, you look refreshed."

"I feel refreshed, Joy. I'm glad you suggested eating in." Pointing to the table by the window, he said, "I picked up a couple of beers." During dinner, Gus asked, "So, how was your day?"

"I had a good day. After you left, I watched the sunrise—simply beautiful—hung out at the pool, visited the mall, then just walked the town. What about your day?"

"Work wasn't too busy, just long. I tried not to disturb you last night, but I was on the phone with one of my mom's sisters for about an hour. She's a talker, and since my mother's death, I've been taking care of her."

When he said that, I remembered again why I took him out of rotation: he never had time because he was taking care of his mom.

Trying to sound concerned, I asked, "Is everything okay?"

"Yes, she's fine. Just like my mom, she loves to chat before bed."

After listening to him talk about his aunt, I started to think he wasn't available for a committed relationship. Like I told my girls, *When you forget why you took someone out of rotation, time will remind you why you stopped dealing with them.*

Following dinner, we went back and chilled in my room for about an hour. On his way to his room, I told him he could close the adjoining door.

When he closed his door, I said, "Damn, that was stressful. Anywho, bye-the-hell-bye."

After I took my shower, I called L. When he answered, he asked, "Do you hear what's playing in the background? Hold on. Let me turn it up." When he came back to the phone, I could hear "Pillow Talk" by Sylvia playing in the background. He whispered, "My sweet Candy . . . damn, I miss you, baby."

Thank goodness he could not see me blushing. When the song was over, I told him to put on The Spinners' "Working My Way Back to You."

He said, "That'll work, too. Baby, my love for you will live from now until the other side of creation." With a sexy whisper, he said, "Baby, remember you're talking to L. You can't scare me off. Call me when you leave town and get back to Atlanta. Hope to see you soon."

The possibility of L coming back into my life made my toes spread. *I am ready to get back home.*

CHAPTER 19

MUFFIN AND COFFEE

Michael

Darren called to let me know he had to extend his trip. Listening to him fumble through his lie, I wanted to tell him, *Fine by me. Winston can handle things.* I wasn't sitting around waiting for my loser husband to want me when this awesome man loves me.

The PJ party was a blast—not to mention the after-PJ party. Dancing, eating, playing cards, and laughing were what this lonely house needed. After the pajama party, Winston and I sat on the sofa. In the middle of our conversation, he fell asleep. Looking at this sleeping work of God, my mind went back to the mountain house in Jamaica and swimming in the nude. My ears heard Rosie telling me to keep in touch with Winston. I woke him up and told him to go to bed.

Lord, I am so tired. Thank goodness my girls cleaned up before leaving.

I smiled when I read the note on the counter: "Good

morning! The coffee maker is ready to go for your drunk, hot ass. P.S. I hope you gave that pussy up. Love, Joy."

Shit, the only thing on my mind was taking a hot shower and getting some sleep.

The next morning, I checked my phone to find a message from Winston: THANKS FOR EVERYTHING. DIDN'T WANT TO WAKE YOU, SO I LET MYSELF OUT. CHECK THE KITCHEN, I LEFT YOU A TREAT.

Rolling out of the bed, I headed to the kitchen in search of my treat. Sitting on the kitchen counter, to my surprise, was my favorite pumpkin muffin and a rose.

I sat at the kitchen table checking my email. Damn, the muffin and coffee seemed to upset my stomach. I had this urge to throw up. I knew I couldn't make it to the trash can. Not wanting to clean up my vomit, I buried my head in the antique vase from Darren's mama and let loose.

My IUD made me bleed last week, so my doctor removed it and prescribed birth control. *Now the pills are giving me hell.* To be honest, I didn't have to worry about making babies. Lately, sleeping with Darren was like sleeping with the dead.

I'm going to stop taking them today. What's the use?

Damn, I need to brush my teeth and wash this ugly-ass vase. Both smell like death.

CHAPTER 20

LAISSEZ LES BON TEMPS ROULER

Joy

In celebration of my promotion to senior executive, Michael and Gypsy planned a dinner party for the next day at Michael's. I don't like mixing work with pleasure, but since it was a work-related celebration, I decided to invite my boss, Karen, and a couple of my coworkers.

Before I left the office, Michael texted, STOP BY THE HOUSE AFTER WORK AND COME IN THROUGH THE GARDEN ENTRANCE.

When I pulled up, the event planners were in the process of setting up lights and a huge white tent with raised floors. The first thing I noticed when I entered the garden was the floating candles in the pool. *Now, how cool is that? Hell, I hope no one gets too drunk and falls in. That would be some Monday morning conversation.*

I guessed one of the workers told Michael I was outside, because she and Gypsy came out smiling and asked, "So, how do you like it?"

"Like it? Ladies, I love it!"

Both gave me a big hug. "Baby, we are so proud of you."

Gypsy handed me a scarf and told me to cover my eyes. With eyes covered, they took my hand and said, "Follow us." When we stopped, Gypsy removed the scarf. I stood in total shock. They had the pool house set up like a five-star restaurant with white tablecloths and white-covered chairs.

In awe, I asked, "So, we are going to eat in here? What is the white tent for?"

Gypsy said, "Honey, that's for the dance floor and DJ. One more surprise: I fixed up the bedroom in the pool house so you all can sleep over after the party."

"Dinner's ready," Michael said after our tour. "Let's hang out in the house and let the team finish setting up." With a glance toward the garage, Michael turned and said, "Damn, Darren's home. Be careful what you say. You know his nosy ass."

When we walked into the kitchen, Darren said, "Looks like you ladies are getting ready for tomorrow's hootenanny."

Michael stopped and just looked at him. Gypsy and I didn't acknowledge his dumb comment. We just greeted him and sat at the kitchen counter. I texted Michael and Gypsy, FORGET HIS LOW-VIBING ASS. STAY IN YOUR HAPPY PLACE. GIVE IT TIME, ONE DAY HE WILL HAVE TO DEAL WITH THE UNEXPECTED CONSEQUENCES OF BEING AN EVIL PIECE OF SHIT.

To change the mood in the room, I started talking about the party. "Ladies, we are going to have a ball. My boss, Karen, promised she would come. I hope so—she's been a little blue since her boyfriend dumped her. After the breakup, she fell into a depression so bad, she had to go on medical leave for three months. She's my biggest advocate. The last thing I need is for her to fall back into depression."

After dinner, Michael asked if we wanted to open a bottle of wine. Pushing back from the counter, I said, "Nope, that is it for me. I have an early-morning meeting." Just to aggravate Darren's stank-ass on my way out, I stopped by the den and said, "See you at the party."

Everybody in the office seemed to be excited about the party, even Karen. At the end of the day, I sent out an email to my team: "I'm on my way out. Looking forward to seeing you all tonight. Come ready to party."

Wanting to greet my guests as they arrived, I decided to get dressed for the party at Michael's. When I got home, I packed an overnight bag, dropped the dogs off at the sitter, picked up my dress from the cleaners, and headed over to Michael's. Pulling up to Michael's house, I saw Gypsy outside talking to the valet that was setting up the valet station.

After I parked, Gypsy walked over to help me with my bags. Giving her a hug, I said, "Damn, Michael is going all out."

Instead of going into the main house, Gypsy followed the cute arrows pointing to the garden. Looking at the final setup, all I could say was, "Amazing." The white tent had a wood-planked dance floor and chandeliers. The DJ stage was set up in the back of the tent. The pool was full of floating candles, and in the entrance of the dining area hung a banner: CONGRATULATIONS, JOY!

When the party kicked off, I was so elated to see everyone from work. Karen seemed to be having a ball. Scanning the room, I saw Darren standing in the background smiling and profiling at my "hootenanny."

What a fucking jerk.

Other than Darren, I enjoyed watching everyone enjoying themselves. After dinner, we all moved to the dance floor.

I really didn't expect to see my coworker Mad Martha. We coined that name because she always looked like she was eating sour gummies. She kept her hair stiff, and I did not know where she got those 1960s dresses. When "Brick House" kicked off the Soul Train line, Mad Martha stood in the line looking like, *WTTF—what the total fuck?* She tried not to dance with anyone. Just as she got to the top of the line, the DJ kicked in "Back That Azz Up!" She started earthquaking that ass. Watching her moves, I concluded she was born with that sour face, because her expression did not change during the entire dance.

When the music slowed down, Darren pulled me on the dance floor. Lucky for him, I was a happy drunk.

After all my coworkers left, we refilled the drinks, fired up some weed, and played a couple of card games. Now, the slow players were playing spades, and us grown folk talked trash while playing Bid Whist. I could tell I was starting to sober up, because when Darren tried to hug me, I pulled back and looked at him like he'd lost his damn mind.

CHAPTER 21

HOW LOW CAN YOU GO?

Joy

Mad Martha was the first person I ran into in the elevator on Monday. Acting like it was just another day at the office, she looked straight ahead and said, "I really enjoyed your party. Took me back to my *American Bandstand* days."

All I could say was, "Thanks so much for coming."

Karen came into the office smiling like a little schoolgirl. Pulling up a chair, she said, "I had a great time. I am so glad I came."

"We all were so glad to have you. Did you have time to network?"

Blushing, she said, "Yes, I did, and I met someone."

"Now, look at you! So, who is the lucky guy?" I teased.

"His name is Mike."

Now, in my mind, I didn't remember a Mike. Maybe he was a guest of a guest. Not giving it much thought, I smiled and told her how happy I was for her.

Every Monday, I could set my watch on her sharing something about Mike. It was good to see her feeling sexy. But after about a month of being love-bombed, she came in looking like someone dropped a bomb on her. Her old smile was gone, her new smile was gone, and she just wasn't smiling at all.

When I asked what was going on, sadly she said, "Mike is starting to act detached, and it's breaking my heart."

One morning she came in looking better. I could see a shadow of her smile. To encourage her, I asked what was up.

"Mike promised to come to my dinner party. I hope he doesn't let me down."

I stood up and hugged her. "I'm sure he'll come through."

After lunch, she stopped by to show off the dress she bought for the party. Before she left, I asked, "Did Mike tell you why he was so detached?"

Smiling like a schoolgirl, she said, "Girl, yes! Last night in bed, with tear-filled eyes, he shared he usually detaches when he falls in love, and he wasn't sure if I felt the same."

Well, I guess that works for her, but for me, it sounds a little shady. Two kicks in the nuts.

All weekend, I was tempted to call Karen, but since she was my boss, I didn't want to have that kind of relationship with her.

First thing Monday morning, Karen stopped by looking like she got a little loving.

"So, girl, tell me about the party. Now, lady, I want to hear from his arrival to his departure," I said.

Sitting on the edge of her seat, she said, "Work had him running an hour late, so he was able to meet my guests, but unfortunately, he got an emergency call from work and had to leave."

To tell you the truth, something about his story just did not sit well with me. So, I asked her where Mike was from. Smiling, she replied, "He lives between Miami and Jamaica."

Now, I was thinking, *I don't remember anyone from Jamaica at the party. Matter of fact, I talked to everyone, and I know damn well I didn't hear anyone say, "Ya, mon."*

Not wanting to burst her bubble, I replied, "Wow, he sounds interesting." However, I thought, *If she likes going for the dumb shit, hell, I'm happy for her.*

Karen would stop by every time she connected with Mike and give me the lowdown.

Based on this psychology article I read, Mike was showing some of the characteristics of a narcissist. Love-bombing was the first red flag—build you up, tear you down, and then abuse you. Each time Karen would stop by, I started checking off the signs.

Late one night, she called. She was in tears. I didn't want to ask, but this time I had to. "Hi, lady, are you okay?"

She didn't respond, so I asked again. Her response just broke me up. "No, I'm not. Mike and I had dinner tonight. When the bill came, he said he left his wallet in the car. I offered to pay, but he angrily refused. When he left the table, I went to the restroom. I sat at the table for about fifteen minutes. I started to worry, so I went outside to check on him."

After she said that, all I heard was the TV in the background, so I knew she was still on the line. I didn't say a word. Finally, she continued, "When I got outside, his car was gone. I went back inside and waited. I thought maybe he went to the ATM. I tried to call, but my calls kept going to his voicemail. I got tired of waiting, so I paid the bill and left."

To make her feel better, I told her, "Don't worry. I'm sure he's okay." After we hung up, the only thing that came to mind was, *Now, he's tearing her down.*

The next morning, she came by smiling like all was good. I dared not ask what his sorry excuse was. She shared Mike was going to meet her for lunch.

Now, I got hot. *His trick ass.* So, I said, "See? I told you he was okay. I'm sure he'll explain everything at lunch."

"Smart girl, that's what he said."

As she was walking out of the door, I asked, "So, where is he taking you?"

"We have reservations at the Red Dragon at noon," she said, smiling.

All I could say was, "Get it, girl."

With all she shared, and me not being able to recall meeting a Mike at my party, I thought it was time for me to put a face to her Mike, and the best time would be now. *I know when and where she's meeting him for lunch. I'm going to sit out front of the restaurant to see if I can get a glimpse of this mystery man.*

I texted Karen to let her know I had to leave at eleven and would be working from home. She responded back with two happy faces. Eleven o'clock could not come fast enough. When I got to my car, I put the address in my GPS and headed to the Red Dragon.

When I got to the restaurant, I found a café right across the street. I checked my phone. *Great, it's 11:30.* The host walked up, smiling, and told me they had just opened and to feel free to seat myself. I scanned the restaurant for a table that faced the front of the Red Dragon, and my eyes locked on the table with a red table cover and glass vase with two small roses.

I sat down and placed my purse in the other chair, then

pulled out my phone to check the time again. I noticed my battery was at 50 percent, looked under the table, and found an outlet right in front of my chair. After I plugged the phone in, the server came over, set the table, and handed me a menu.

I thought, *I better order something.* Before he left, I ordered a double shot of whiskey.

While I buried my head in the menu, I heard a car door slam right in front of where I was sitting. Slowly, I peeked over the menu, and I saw Karen walking across the street. I recalled the windows of the café were tinted, so I knew it was safe for me to come out of hiding. Just as Karen was about to open the door into the restaurant, she turned around like someone had called her name. Instead of walking into the restaurant, she turned, smiled, and walked away.

My eyes followed her down the sidewalk. When I locked my eyes on the man, I almost tipped over the table. I snatched my phone off the charger and zoomed in on the man. When he came into focus, all I could say was, "What the hell!" My hands trembled, I started sweating, and I knew fire was coming out of my ass and nose. Then I hit record.

That little skunk—her *Mike* was Darren.

It took all I could not to run across the street and dropkick him right between his eyes. I watched him greet her with a kiss, then he put his arm around her, opened the door, and ushered her in.

Wait, so that's why he stayed in the background until my coworkers left the party! He was stalking Karen, and it explains why he tried to hug me when I was playing cards . . . he was working his plan.

By this time, I had kicked off one of my shoes. The

server came over with my drink and asked if I had decided on lunch. Before he put the drink down, I snatched it out of his hand and just threw it back. I ordered something to eat, then I ordered another double.

About an hour later, I saw Darren and Karen come out, and again I started to record. I watched him hold the door for her. I watched them jaywalk across the street to her car. Before he opened her door, they stood there and kissed. When she got into the car and drove off, I recorded his nothing-ass until he turned the corner.

When the coast was clear, I paid my bill and ran out, but before I hit the sidewalk, I called Gypsy.

No answer? Where in the hell is she? I kept calling her; I was too pissed to leave a message.

When I got to the car, I tried one more time. This time she picked up. I said, "Girl, where are you?"

Before answering, she said, "What's going on?"

Trying to keep my cool, I asked again, "Where are you?" My tone told her not to ask me anything, just to answer me. "Girl, do you have some weed?"

"Weed? Girl, are you blowing my phone up for some damn weed?"

"Hell no! I got something to show you. Meet me at my house in fifteen minutes."

When I got home, she was standing at the front door. I didn't say hello; I just walked in like she wasn't standing there. Not saying a word, she followed me to the kitchen. All I could do was hand her my phone. I narrated the video while she watched. When the video was over, she just gave me a blank look.

Gypsy asked, "What in the hell is he up to?"

Talking through my teeth, I said, "I bet he heard me tell you all about how fragile Karen is. She's my mentor, and if he gets her all jacked up, I'm sure she'll have a breakdown. I can't speak for his actions. Maybe he's pissed the party went so well, or he thinks if Karen isn't around to support me, I'll fall. I don't know. I am not that low-down to think like him."

Feeling bad for me, Gypsy asked, "Joy, that is some low-down bull. What are you going to do?"

All I could say was, "Other than felonious assault, I don't know."

When Gypsy handed me my phone, I noticed it was one thirty. I forgot I had a two o'clock conference call with Karen. I ran out to the car to get my laptop.

Karen sounded like she was on cloud nine during the conference call. Before she hung up, I told her I wasn't feeling well, and I was going to end my day early.

I walked back into the kitchen with Gypsy. "Girl, how could someone use people the way he does? Karen's going to be devastated. If Michael knew about this, it would hurt her—not the cheating, but his attempt to hurt me. I'm not going to give him the pleasure of hurting Michael, so telling her is not in the equation. That little narcissistic bastard. Damn. Gypsy, when I realized it was Darren, I wanted to drop-kick his teeth down his throat and drown him in the sewer."

When I said that, Gypsy fell to the floor screaming, "Jesus, please take the wheel. Joy, calm down. Breathe and go lie down on the sofa in the den."

Gypsy was right. Soon as I stepped into the den, I started to release all the negative energy of the day. Lying on the sofa, I started to think about how this room had been our safe place, our think tank, our free zone, the place where unconditional sista love was shared. If these walls could talk, it'd tell the good, the bad, and the lonely.

Before I knew it, I was waking up to the sound of something playing on the TV.

Damn, my brain feels like it's been spinning for hours. Looking at my phone, I saw Gypsy left me a message telling me she would pick up TJ and Maxx from doggie daycare and would be back over at seven with dinner.

After I read her message, I dropped my arms, fell back on the sofa, and went back to sleep.

The message from my security system woke me up. Pulling the phone to my face, I saw someone in my driveway; I watched the lady driver step out and disappear behind the raised trunk. I dropped the phone and headed to the front door. When I got there, the lady was standing at the bottom of the steps with a breathtaking arrangement of flowers.

She handed me the flowers and said, "Looks like someone is thinking of you."

My eyes moved from the flowers to the card sitting next to the largest white rose.

I placed the flowers on the table next to the window in the den, stood back, and let the beauty caress my eyes. Sitting on the sofa, I slowly opened the card, thinking they for sure came from Gus. But the card didn't say, "Thinking about you," or "I hope you are having a lovely day." It just said, "Sweet Candy."

Those two words touched and warmed my soul, stimulated my mind, and softened my cold, cold heart.

Gypsy pulled in the driveway with TJ sitting in the front seat looking straight ahead, pinning Maxx behind him. When she parked, I heard her scream, "Damn, can y'all wait? Get the hell off me!" By this time, TJ was standing in her lap and Maxx was jumping on TJ. When she finally opened the door, both dogs ran to the grass to potty.

By the time she got to the front of the car, TJ got in front of her. When Maxx finished, he got behind her. Now they were in formation. As expected, I heard Gypsy screaming, "TJ, speed up. Maxx, stop jumping on the back of my legs."

When they reached the front door, TJ stood wagging his tail, and Maxx was jumping on the door barking his head off. Gypsy, at the bottom of the steps, was holding dinner and looking pissed.

Before opening the door, I screamed, "Maxx, I told you to stop knocking on this door like you the damn police."

When I stepped out to help Gypsy, TJ and Maxx ran in. Handing me the bags, Gypsy said, "These two mofos are crazy, just like their mama."

When we got into the house, TJ was peeking around the door. I told her, "Hurry, go the other way." We both knew what was on TJ's mind.

Putting my finger to my mouth, we tip-toed through the dining room. I peeked through the slat in the folding doors and saw Maxx walking off. While we were standing there, that damn Maxx came up from behind us and just started barking like we were burglars. When I opened the folding door, there was TJ. We just fell into formation, TJ walking and looking back, me holding the food, and Maxx in the back jumping on the back of Gypsy's legs.

Gypsy spotted the flowers. "So, Gus is still at it?"

Smiling, I said, "Nope. They came from an old friend."

Hugging me, she asked, "Does he have a brother?"

Later, while eating, she asked, "What is your plan of action for Darren?"

"Well, we agreed we can't tell Michael, and we for sure can't tell Karen. From where I'm sitting, I have the game advantage. I need to be up close and personal with her, keep her focused until this plays out, and after that, I'm going to help her through this madness. Now, Darren will hang himself. Watch. I know what he's up to, but he doesn't know what I'm up to."

Then I told her, "Let's invoke the forty-five-minute fuckery rule: forty-five minutes to deal with negative energy. As far as I'm concerned, we passed forty-five minutes hours ago. Let's not spend another second on this evil."

While cleaning the kitchen, Gypsy said, "I love the way you smiled when you looked at your flowers. Are you ready to give this special person a name?"

When she said that, I thought, *See, this is how a real girlfriend handles things. Now, the nosy mofos would jump into it, but this classy queen asked how I felt about sharing. I so love my girls. Thanks, God.*

I said, "Sure, come back over tomorrow. This is going to be a long story."

CHAPTER 22

WHAT!

Joy

I invited Gypsy over the next day to give her the backstory about the flowers. Just as I finished making a tray of appetizers, I heard the dogs barking and saw Gypsy standing at the door through my security system. I hollered from the kitchen, "Come in! The door's open."

When she walked into the kitchen, she said, "Next time you go to therapy, take these fools. You know that damn TJ wouldn't let me pass him. When I tried to, he growled at me, and Maxx's little ass started barking—I guess to make me stay in formation."

"You might be right. The dog pound in therapy? Now, that would be a hoot. Gypsy, girl, calm down and go get my pipe out of the den and grab that bottle of whiskey."

While placing the bottle and pipe on the kitchen table, she said, "Girl, I have to say it again—these flowers are great. Love them!"

"They are lovely." I handed her the lighter and a glass.

"Fire this up and make the drinks, because I'm getting ready to tell you a secret and mind-blowing truth."

"Girl, about who? Gus?"

I said, "Gus? Honey, now he's a nephew-husband."

When I said that, Gypsy started to act like she fainted.

"Girl, get your ass up. He's taking care of his aunt. Forget his ass." Changing the subject, I said, "I need to tell you something. I think I saw Darren while I was in Jacksonville."

"Are you sure? Joy, your old eyes are playing tricks on you. Michael called me to tell me he had a business meeting somewhere in South Georgia. All I know, she was somewhat disappointed."

"Why was she disappointed? She should be glad to be rid of him."

Gypsy told me, "Well, she said he had planned the trip earlier in the year, and she was planning on going down with him, but at the last minute—or should I say the last second—she had shopped for the trip when he told her there was a change in plans and she couldn't attend the meeting."

"Gypsy, that lying piece of shit. I'm pretty sure while I was out shopping in Jacksonville, I saw Darren with this white girl. I was too far away, but I'm not that blind. Later I saw the girl, so I followed her to a store. It threw me because it looked like she had this unique engagement ring on. The design was different. I knew I'd seen it before, but I just didn't know where—"

"Joy, stop. He was not in Jacksonville. He was on St. Simon's Island, Georgia. Forget what you thought you saw. Your eyes and mind were playing tricks on you." Then Gypsy said, "Stop talking about him. Let's talk about the flowers."

"Okay, you're right. Now, this is going to take a minute, so stay with me. For you to really understand the backstory, I'm going to have to give you the bloody details. I remember this story like it just happened."

Excited, Gypsy said, "I have all evening."

I sat down, took my drink, and began, "You know, I grew up fast."

With her undivided attention, Gypsy replied, "If that's what you want to call it, I'm good with that. Just keep talking."

"Girl, I learned early in life how to handle myself around the fast men. I am not talking about the young knuckleheads who only thought about lying on their dicks. I am talking about the young men that were turned out at twelve by their twenty-two-year-old babysitters. In a way, we could connect because we both saw or experienced things that we should have waited for. These special man-children always took a liking to me. While girls my age liked the boys with the new sneakers, I liked the baby players with their gators, pinky rings, and purty white smiles.

"Like every teenager, I had a crew. Mine consisted of two of my classmates from my neighborhood, Brandy and Terri. The three of us were spoiled to the core: new cars, shopping trips at will, all the best weed, and free as the wind. Even though we were the same age, my thought process was ten years ahead of their parents' and light years ahead of my crew. To be honest, I enjoyed playing Bid Whist with their parents more than hanging out with them.

"One weekend, while hanging out at Terri's house, in came the force that would change my life and every young boy's life around me forever: Terri's cousin L, from Memphis."

With a puzzled brow, Gypsy asked, "Was that his name, just L?"

"Yep, just L. His full name is L Blackfoot. Tall, teeth white like eggshells, slicked-back hair black as the darkest night and his shoes polished. Now, I learned early you could tell what kind of man you're dealing with by his shoes and hair. Unkept shoes? Just a lazy ass. Hair parted on the side? A pretty mama's boy. Parted in the middle? A target. Combed to the front? A coon. Slicked back? A taught player."

Mouth opened, Gypsy asked, "Where in the hell do you get this shit from?"

"Hanging around the right crowd." I continued, "When L was over, he had limited conversation with Terri and Brandy, but with me, the conversation and questions never ended. One night, playing cards with Terri's parents, I grooved to 'Sexy Mama' by the Moments. When I looked up to place my bid, I caught L looking my way. When our eyes locked, he flashed that white smile. Being me, I did not smile back.

"After the game, I walked into the kitchen to find him sitting at the counter. While I fixed my plate, he started the conversation. 'Ms. Joy, so you finally had to give up your seat. I can tell you like playing.'

"I replied, 'Yes, I learned the game young. I really enjoy playing. Something about beating, the self-proclaimed master of the game makes me click my heels.'

"With a look of intrigue, he asked, 'So do you consider yourself a master?'

"All I said was, 'Not yet.'

"'So, Ms. Joy, I noticed you're the only one in your little crew that doesn't have a boyfriend.'

"I told him, 'I have no interest in *boys*. They're cool to

hang out with, but the way these girls are fooling around with them is appalling to me.'

"When I said that, he stood up and asked, 'Baby girl, please tell me you're not gay.'

"I replied, 'Hell no. That is *not* what I am saying. My point is these little boys know nothing about themselves, so how in the hell would they know about dealing with a young queen like me?'

"He didn't respond, and I didn't help him. When I heard there was an open spot at the card table, I finished up and walked out of the kitchen, leaving him sitting still like a statue."

Sitting in silence, I felt a happy tear run down my cheek. I looked at Gypsy and said, "For me to really give you the blow by blow, I need my diary. I'm going to share a few special moments I never shared with anyone." Reaching for the purple diary next to the flowers with a large letter "L" in the middle of a red heart, I brought Gypsy on a ride down memory lane.

"All our parents were out of town one weekend," I read aloud. "During that time, leaving a sixteen-year-old home alone was not an issue. Taking advantage of her situation, Terri invited a bunch of boys over. While Terri and her friends were doing what I guess kids did, I hung out in the kitchen making pizza and cookies. I took my shower, then I came back to an empty house. Well, the den was empty, but the bedroom doors were locked.

"While I was cooking, I heard the front door open, and in came L. Instead of sitting down, he walked up behind me and gave me a big hug. 'So, Ms. Joy, where is everyone?'

"Instead of responding, I asked, 'Where have you been?'

"Looking at me like a nasty old man, he said, 'So, you missed me?'

"I waited a couple of seconds and reached for the towel, pulled the pizza out of the oven, placed a slice in front of him, and said, 'Let me know what's missing.'

"Girl, when he picked up that pizza, I knew then he would eat whatever I put in front of him.

"Looking around the room, he said, 'Really, where are your sidekicks?'

"Not looking up from the cookie batter, I simply replied, 'I guess they're back there fooling around with those little nasty dick boys.'

"About that time, all of them came out looking like they all saw a ghost. Terri knew she was in trouble, but she just played it off by introducing her friends to L. The look he gave them must have scared them off because they left without eating. Terri made small talk, then she and Brandy left. On their way out, he told them to set the alarm before leaving and to call when him when they were on their way back home.

"After he heard the alarm set, L got up and placed his plate in the sink. Before I knew it, he was standing behind me—I mean, standing *right* behind me. When I moved, he said, 'So, what's wrong?'

"I replied, 'Do want to try some of my cookies?'

"Looking like a little boy, he said, 'Ms. Joy, you are a piece of work.'

"He went into the den and sat on the floor next to the sofa. With the remote in hand, he went through the channels until he landed on an old black-and-white movie. I heard him scream, 'This is my favorite movie!'

"After I finished the cookies, I joined him. Did my hot butt sit on the chair across from the sofa? No. I sat on the sofa, close enough for my leg to touch his shoulder and to slide a cookie in his mouth. Rubbing the outside of my leg, he said, 'If you don't want to watch this, we can change the channel.'

"'The movie is fine. I love anything made by Hitchcock.' I lit a joint, reached down, and placed it between his kissable lips.

"Jesus, take the wheel. Before the first commercial, he kissed my legs until they rested on his wide shoulders. By the time he reached the top of my thighs, my panties were behind his head. His head was buried so deep, all I could do was pull his ears.

"In the middle of his dirty deed, he asked, 'Are you a virgin?'

"With a shaky voice and closed eyes, I said, 'Yes.'

"Kissing the inside of my thighs, he softly whispered, 'Baby, stay that way.' When he finished, he slid my panties off, rubbed them on my young, wet pussy, and stuffed them into his pocket.

"After the movie, he talked about his plans for moving down to Miami. He kissed me and whispered, 'Promise to stay my sweet Candy until then,' and from that moment on, I went from Joy to Candy.

"On his way out, he handed me two hundred-dollar bills under a half-eaten cookie. I never mentioned this to anyone. Over the weekend, he stopped by a couple more times, but he never tried to kiss, touch, or stand close behind me.

"Two months later, L bought a place on the beach, and the crew had an open invitation. When I stopped by Terri's house one day, she told me there was a free beach concert near L. She called him to tell him we were taking him up on his offer. He gave us the code to the gate, and we headed out.

"When we got to the gate, of course, Terri forgot the

code. After the third try, the gate finally opened. When we were unpacking the car, out of nowhere water dropped out of the sky. Now, we all knew it wasn't raining. Like little robots, we looked straight up."

With a quick glance up from the diary, I asked, "And who did we see standing on the balcony with a water bottle tipped over in his hand?"

Gypsy replied, "L?"

"You got it. L." I continued, "In the elevator, Terri tried to enter the code again, but her mascara had started to run and she couldn't see a damn thing. I pushed her out of the way and took control. On our way up, we discussed how we were going to gang up and throw him off the balcony.

"We all were expecting the doors to open to some long-carpeted hallway, but to our surprise, we stepped right into his paradise decked out all in white, from the floor to the sofa pillows. The sunlight from the large window made the room look almost blinding.

"Terri asked for a towel to wipe her face off. I reached over and handed her the white throw from the back of the sofa and said, 'Girl, use this.'

"After we cleaned up, L gave Terri a concert pass for her to get into the VIP section. It wasn't long before Terri and Brandy were standing in the elevator half-naked, glasses in hand, and giggling like the little girls they were. I told them I would join them later.

"Standing at the window, I could see the crew making their way to the concert. L left the room and came back with this white box with a lovely, big red bow. I didn't open it. Instead, I sat it on the table and continued to look out of the window. He said nothing, and I did nothing.

"Finally, I walked away from the window and headed for the kitchen. I noticed again how clean everything was.

The kitchen looked like four women lived there. Just as I opened the fridge, he stood behind me like he did when I was making cookies. This time I didn't move. When he held me, I felt us becoming one.

"Before I knew it, he picked me up and placed me on the counter. His head found its way to my treasure. Like the last time, he kept my panties.

"When I started to jump off the counter, he told me to stay put while he ordered lunch. Reaching in the drawer under my hips, he pulled out this menu and said, 'What ya want?' After he placed our orders, he kissed me and said, 'Girl, get your nasty little butt off my counter.'

"While we were on the balcony, the doorbell rang. I followed L to the elevator. When the doors opened, a guy pushing a white table came in, set up the table outside on the balcony, and left.

"After lunch, we talked about my upcoming graduation plans. When I told him I was going to FAMU, he stopped breathing. 'Wait, in Tallahassee? I thought you were going to the community college. Baby, you're only sixteen.'

"I thought, *I never told him that. What does sixteen have to do with it?* I said to L, 'I need to wrap up this phase of my life and move on.'

"Leaving me on the sofa, he got up and walked to the window and just stood there. He reached into his pocket and pulled out a joint. With a slow hand, he lit it and held his head back as the smoke surrounded his head.

"I walked slowly behind him and just held him tight. For a moment he didn't turn around and just softly and slowly rubbed my clenching fingers. When he turned to kiss me, he stopped and soaked in the sunlight shining on my naked body.

"He didn't react like I thought he would. Instead of kissing me, he pushed me back. I walked backward, until I felt the pillows from the white sofa press into the back of my legs. Now, I wouldn't let him punk me, so I just laid back and picked up the remote on the glass table and turned on the TV.

"Standing over me, he reminded me I was sixteen and he was twenty. *So, the rabbit has the gun. Are you going to run, or are you going to get shot?* I thought.

"Instead of walking toward me, he slowly headed to the elevator and locked the doors. I could smell his man scent mixed with his cologne as he stood behind me. I could hear him undress. In the TV, I saw the reflection of his naked body. My eyes led me to the beauty that hung in front of him.

"We played around, but we never had sex. He told me after I graduated, we would see where we went. This time, he touched my young, tender breasts, and then he worked his way back down to my treasure. When he finished, he went back to his joint.

"Later, we went down to the beach, where we found Terri and Brandy surrounded by a bunch of nasty old men.

"After the concert, we hung out with L for a while. On our way out, he walked us to the car, and before I got in, he slid five hundred-dollar bills in my back pocket.

"Later, when I graduated high school, my family and friends were there to cheer me on, but I saw L hanging in the background while we were outside taking pictures. Later that night, Terri and Brandy wanted to go to some graduation parties, but we went over to hang out with L before hitting the streets. I wanted to stay where I was, so I lied and told them I would hook up with them later.

"After they left, I settled in, and L kicked off the

evening. First, we went down to the beach. This guy came up wearing white gloves and holding a glass tray with two glasses. A while later, the same guy came down to tell us dinner was ready. When we got back to his place, candles were lit, and the same guy guided us to the table, and dinner was served. I wondered how the other graduation parties were going.

"By the time we finished, I realized we were the only ones in his condo. When I walked to the window, I noticed the white box on the table, the same one he gave me the night of the concert. This time I opened it, and to my surprise, it was a lovely pinky ring. He placed the ring on my finger and gave me a long kiss.

"We became one twice—first with his tongue, then his shame. This went on for a couple of weeks. I never knew how L was making his money, but he made it, and I spent it. The more he gave, the more I wanted."

Placing the diary back on the table, I said, "Now, I was no fool. I knew I had to get out of town. The way I was feeling, I wasn't going to make it to FAMU. So, I decided to move to Tallahassee and start college that summer.

"I guess L really missed me, because every now and then he would come to visit. I appreciated the company of a real man. I must say, those college boys were young, dumb, and full of cum. As time moved on, L's visits grew less frequent. I was good with that; my daddy did not raise a fool.

"But when I graduated college, I looked through the crowd of happy parents for mine. I saw them—and I also saw L. After graduation, I told him I accepted a job with IBM, and I was getting married. It was obvious he was living well, but I knew our lifestyles were different. He was committed to the game, and I was committed to my future.

"Over dinner, he told me, 'You will never be happy with a square, Ms. Candy. You will marry many boys but love only one man.'

"Somewhere in my mind, I knew he was right. But forget it, I was going to give it a shot."

When I finished my story, Gypsy said, "That is some heavy stuff. If it were today, he would be in jail."

Smiling, I said, "Only if I told. We damn sho' was not going to get caught."

"Joy, to be honest, I think that explains why you have never been able to commit to anyone. You're still in love with L."

I tried not to cry, but the tears just started to flow. "Correct. I never stopped loving him. After him, everybody caught hell with me trying to love me." Fixing another round of drinks, I said, "Gypsy, I told you all of that to tell you about my weekend."

"So, what happened?"

"When I was having lunch, I saw this fine man sitting at the bar. He was looking at me, and I was checking him out. When I looked up, he was gone, but before I knew it, I felt this hand touch my shoulder, and when he walked in front of me it was the love of my life."

"Girl, stop. Love at first sight?"

"Well, kind of, but the first sight was twenty-five years ago. The man standing in front of me was the man that took my virginity."

"Hold up, you mean the guy that you just told me about?" Gypsy asked.

"Yep—L. Baby, he looked like a bronze statue. Simply lovely, still smooth, still smelled like magic. Now, check this out. He told me he has been keeping up with me, and he knew how many times I've been married. He sat with me, and we went for a walk afterward. Funny, he had my number. I'm sure he got it from his cousin.

"While I was walking away, he asked me not to get married on him again. After I got back to the hotel, Gus wanted to go to dinner, and you know where he wanted to go? The same restaurant where I had lunch. So, we had dinner by the pool at the hotel. It broke my heart because I could tell he really wanted to be together, but after seeing L, the game changed."

Gypsy said, "Now wait, are you telling me you are going to just throw things away because you ran into an old flame? If I can remember, your MO is 'An ex is an ex for a reason.'"

"But L is not and has never been an ex. He is more than that; he is a relationship that never ended. It was just placed on hold," I said.

"I get that, but how can you come to this just because he asked you not to get married? Honey, please. You better stick with what you know."

I said, "Well, that night in the hotel, he called me and just spilled his heart out, asked me to give him a chance to make things right, to allow him to finish what he started, to bring my love out. I *must* go with my heart. So, I am going to see where it goes. I must. I have to before I die. I have to be the better me."

When I finished, I just held my head in my hands. "L sent the flowers. Gypsy, I am so confused."

Gypsy replied, "I thought you said you never go back to an old dog?"

Shaking my head, I said, "But he isn't an old dog. He's a missing dog that found his way home."

CHAPTER 23

LIVING-ROOM SOFA

Michael

For the life of me, I didn't have a clue where my phone was.

I wish my phone would ring or a lovely person would call. Lord, I hope I didn't turn off the ringer. I bet if I stopped looking, it'd find me. No need to be a slave to the phone. I need an upgrade anyway, so it is what it is.

Wait, I hear it ringing. It is coming from the living room . . . but where?

By the time I finished tearing up the room, the phone had stopped ringing. While in the kitchen, the phone rang again. *I can't believe I'm playing hide-and-seek with a freaking phone.* A video of me running around the room like a crazy woman would go viral.

This room was lovely, but what a waste of space. I never understood what the formal living room was for. A formal dining area is awesome for hosting large parties, but when we had guests, we would guide them to the family room, or we'd all sit in the kitchen. I could remember when I shared the house blueprint, Darren lost it when I didn't consider a formal living room.

If I'd had my way, I would've opened this wall up to make it more inviting. Instead, it looked like you'd need to wear a ball gown and tux before you could sit in there.

I had three missed calls from Darren's mom. Well, not a bad day; I got one of my two wishes. The phone did ring, but I missed out on the lovely-person wish.

Girl, stop. She is sweet, just fake. Her son makes her crazy.

What a perfect place to call her back: sitting on the sofa. I propped my feet on the glass table and called her back.

Good, the phone's going to voicemail. "Hi, love. Sorry I missed your call! I hope all is well. Please call me back. Talk to you later." She knew my voice, so no need to leave my name.

All she does is pressure me about getting pregnant, and she has the balls to act like I have pussy problems. I wanted to tell her, "Your mommy-made son has problems with pussy." She would just roll over if she knew I had not had sex with him in a year. That's right. You only make love with someone you love. Winston showed me that.

Girl, stop. You are sounding like Joy.

I had never seen such a bunch of dysfunctional, materialistic Black people in my life. It killed me how they wore being damn near white like it was a badge of honor. The thought of me bringing a child into this family repulsed me. If I did get pregnant, I hoped my baby would come out looking like the side of the family they tried to hide.

Her only child is a loser, and she is lost and turned out.

Now, what got me was, they were quick to tell you they were West Indian. Every time she said that, I wanted to scream, "Ya ass is Black! Your ancestors were traded for sugar and coconuts. They are slaves and still on the plantation, but instead of picking cotton, they are buying the cotton. When you worship the demons of vanity, material things, status, and drugs, you are still a slave."

What also got me, they were quick to look their noses down on my catering crew. I wanted to tell them my friends were not slaves.

Damn, this sofa is so comfy. The next time Darren is out of town, I am going to put on my PJs, splurge on a large pizza, grab my blanket, and crash on this fancy sofa.

The only person in that family that had good sense was Darren's other grandmother, Rosie.

Rosie was down to earth, free-spirited, and a piece of work. Tall, beautiful, a lady inside and out. She was known to tell it like it was. Now, when she got to drinking and smoking weed, all the family's dirty laundry hit the floor, from Mama's baby and Dad's maybe, to cousins marrying cousins. Her passion was her rose garden, and she truly loved the Caribbean islands, especially the mountains of Jamaica.

I still miss her. She was the only one that had a moral compass.

It used to be that every chance we got, Rosie and I would spend alone time together and just let it all hang out. I never forgot how right after Darren and I got married, she asked me to join her on one of her getaways.

A couple of years ago, Rosie called me out of the blue and asked me to join her on another trip. Without hesitation, I said, "On my way."

Rosie said, "Pack light. We will shop when you get here."

On my way to the airport, I called Gypsy and Joy to let them know my whereabouts, then I called Rosie. "Hey, lady, I'm boarding. See ya when I get there."

When I said that, Rosie broke out singing.

First-class seat! That damn Rosie is one classy sis. When the plane took off, I sat looking at the plane break through the clouds and wondered how it felt to fly free. Something about flying into Jamaica was so captivating: seeing the shadow of the plane flying over the ocean, the mountains, the beaches—just nothing but simple awesomeness.

When I walked off the plane, Rosie was standing there looking like she owned the ground she was standing on. Her white hair looked like a halo next to her tanned skin. As we got closer, we both smiled, like two stars greeting the moonlight.

Our transportation was waiting at the curb. As we approached, this tall man, black as the night, opened the back-seat door. The way he was looking at Rosie, I knew he was not just her car driver.

"Winston, this is my grandbaby, Michael."

With this smooth Jamaican-British accent, he said, "I heard so much about you. Welcome."

Looking out of the window, I noticed we were driving away from the beach and up into the mountains. When we turned off this winding dirt road, to our right was a large waterfall. I rolled the window down. I just had to hear what my eyes were seeing.

The road ended right in front of this white villa with a view that was simply breathtaking. After we parked, Winston opened the car doors for Rosie and me. When we got to the house, Winston introduced me to the staff then escorted us to the patio where we all enjoyed lunch, including the staff. Now, Darren's mama, she would have made the staff eat in the kitchen, even Ms. Wonda.

While I was there, we shopped, swam in the river, and took long walks up to the top of the mountain. Nothing touristy, just local fun. One night, Rosie and I sat out on the patio drinking and smoking. Rosie started going down memory lane. She told me that she and Winston were childhood sweethearts and wanted to marry.

"Why didn't you?" I asked.

"Well, truth be told," Rosie said, "my parents wouldn't allow it, because Winston couldn't pass the paper-bag test." Whenever Rosie would say, "Truth be told," I knew what followed would be hidden truth, lies uncovered, and people revealed.

"What?"

Rosie told me her family had a rule: If he was darker than a paper bag, he was not going to be in the family. She said her family had her husband already picked.

"Had him *picked*?"

"Yes, baby girl. That is how I married Darren's granddad. His family was rich and high-high yellow. During that time, you did as you were told, so I married him, and from day one I felt like a caged rat. He was just as miserable. I was not his pick for a wife. He, too, had someone in mind, but she couldn't pass the test, either." Then she said, "We made it work for the family, but we were miserable.

"Now, don't get me wrong. We were the best of friends, but he was a horrible husband, and I was a horrible wife. We found our own paths to happiness, but we never had joy. After the birth of our son, Darren's father, we started to live separate lives.

"Winston never married. His wife was money. He made a lot, but he knew it couldn't give him joy. He did have a son, though—he's also called Winston, and he's coming in tomorrow from Atlanta, so you all will get a chance to meet.

"After my husband died, Winston and I rekindled our

relationship, and we have been together for over twenty years. Baby, that is why I am always encouraging you to move from happy and run to joy."

The next day, we all went to the airport to pick up Winston's son, Winston Jr. We all greeted the son at the gate. From the smile on Winston's face, he must have spotted his son. It touched my heart to see the love between the three of them.

Rosie did the introductions: "Winston, this is my baby girl, Michael. And Michael, this is my baby boy, Winston."

Looking me straight in my eyes, he said, "Well, a lady called Michael. Now, that's different."

Trying hard not to blush, I said, "Okay, we have Winston and Winston."

Rosie said, "I tell you what. You can call daddy Winston, Uncle Winston, and we will call the son, Winston."

When we got to the car, the driver came around and gave Winston a big hug. "My boy, how have you grown."

Rosie, Uncle Winston, and Winston piled in the back seat. I enjoyed listening to them reminiscing about Winston's childhood. Soon as we reached the house, Winston jumped out of the car, held his hands to the sky, and said, "Nothing like the mountain air."

After lunch, Rosie and Uncle Winston left for the day. I spent the morning sitting out on the patio. Winston came out holding two large buckets. "Hey, I am going down to the river," he said. "Do you want to join me?"

Without answering, I just hopped up, and we both headed for the hills.

As we walked, I asked what the buckets were for.

"Baby, you're in paradise. You never know what you will come across that is simply delicious. Girl, be a part of the memory. Take one of these buckets. Let's see what you come up with."

We walked down the hill and passed the waterfall and river at the end of the road. We took this trail down to the water. When we got to the waterfall, he started to take all his clothes off and just jumped in.

"Winston, are you crazy? Get your tail out of that water!" Before I finished, he disappeared, running along the river. "Winston! Winston, stop playing."

Without warning, he popped up right next to me. I sat on the rocks and watched him swim on top of the water, then he would disappear and end up by the waterfall.

Sitting there, I thought, *Why am I watching fun? I should join the fun!* Before I knew it, I took off all my clothes and jumped in.

Winston said, "Come on, let's catch dinner."

"How are we going to do that?" I asked. "We don't have poles."

I followed him back over to the other side. With both buckets, we were able to catch a shitload of fish. On our way back home, we picked all types of herbs, fruits, and veggies.

When we got back to the house, Winston showed me how to clean the fish, and as we worked, he shared his childhood memories of coming to the island. "I've been coming to this house since I was a baby," he shared. "My mama passed away during childbirth, and Rosie has been the only mother that I've known. But in respect for my mother, Rosie refers to herself as my godmother, but I know she loves me like she had me."

Puzzled, I asked, "Do you have any memories of Darren in Jamaica?"

"No, not really. Funny, Rosie never encouraged a

relationship between the two of us, and the only time I saw him was if he happened to visit Rosie in Georgia. You know, I always thought it was strange that Rosie never invited him to Jamacia. If you noticed, all the pictures in the house are of me through the years. She keeps Darren's pictures in a drawer in the hallway."

After dinner, Winston and his dad went for a walk. While they were out, Rosie started going down memory lane again. She started off with, "Baby, I fell in love with you the first time Darren brought you over, but it broke my heart to see you getting tied down to him. Yes, he is my only grand, but he is so much like his mother, it makes my heart cold." She reached for my hand and just placed her ring on my finger. Looking at the ring, she said, "This is our secret."

All I could do was cry. "Thank you for being my friend," I finally said.

"Baby girl, follow me. I have something to show you."

By this time, both of us were walking sideways, but so what?

As we walked down the long hallway to her office, I noticed how tastefully decorated her home was. I had never ventured this deep into her house in paradise. We stopped in front of these large double doors. She opened one side, and I opened the other. As soon as we walked into the room, the lights came on. In the middle of the room was a large mahogany desk. She gestured for me to sit in the black-leather chair next to the desk. Before sitting down, she opened the desk drawer with the key that she had in her bra. Reaching in, she pulled out a yellow envelope.

Rosie said, "Baby, I'm sharing this with you. Do not—and I mean *do not*—share this with a soul. Now, my grandson and his mama think I'm broke. Just because I don't show what I have does not mean I'm broke." Slowly, she pinched the metal tab on the envelope and pulled out a stack of papers. "This is my will. My lawyers have been directed to contact you and Winston in private after my death." Handing me the papers, she said, "I'm leaving you and Winston everything that I have. Don't mention this to Darren."

I must have looked stunned, because she said, "Baby, are you okay?"

"Yes, I am—but why me?"

"Why not? I've watched you over the years. You are too good for those people. If I leave anything to Darren, he will waste it on his mama or on dope."

Stunned again, I replied, "Dope?"

"Yes, he's a dope head."

"Rosie, do you know this for sure?"

Looking at me like, *You poor little fool*, she said, "In the last year, I had someone check him out, and based on the report given, he's a dope head just like his mama is a drunk. To be honest, I really don't think that's my son's child."

In shock, I said, "Rosie, hold on. What makes you think that?"

"Let me put it like this. My son used to say, 'That boy doesn't look like anybody I know.' That's why Darren was never allowed to call him 'Daddy.'"

All I could say was, "Well, damn. I often wondered why he referred to him as 'Father' and not 'Daddy.'"

"Correct. My son would say, 'I'm not his daddy. I'm what the birth certificate says I am: father.' That's one reason why I never gave a damn about him not visiting."

With this caring look on her face, she said, "Baby girl,

promise me and yourself to find the strength to leave him. You deserve better." She took the papers, placed them back in the envelope, put them back in her desk, and locked the drawer. When she stood up, she came around the desk and handed me the key.

What she said next made me pause. "When you become single, I want you to spend more time with Winston. He's a good man, just like his dad."

So sad—a year to the day of our conversation, her plans were carried out, and to this day Darren knows nothing about the trust she left me. Funny, he thinks I get my pocket change from my catering business. Rosie was right. What a loser.

At her funeral, the dark people sat on one side, and the lost souls sat on the other. For the hell of it, I came late, so I found a reason not to sit with their fake asses. Now, what pissed me off: Darren sat over there crying his eyes out, and I know for sure he gave less than a damn about her. When we walked past for the final viewing, I leaned over, gave her a kiss, and at the same time, I slid a joint in the casket.

At the internment, Darren had the nerve to ask her lawyer about her estate. The lawyer's response almost made me fall in the grave. "Darren, your grandmother's estate was settled before she passed. You will not be needed."

Since I drove alone, I stayed at the gravesite until they buried her. While sitting there, I heard someone sit right next to me. It was her lawyer. Under his breath, he said, "Did you hear that little motherfucker ask about her estate?" Then he introduced himself and handed me his card. He told me Rosie took care of everything before she died and asked me to stop by his office on Monday, early if possible.

Monday morning, when I arrived at his office, his

secretary escorted me to this large conference room. I sat there for about ten minutes, then he and another attorney came in with a large folder. After the introductions, he handed me her will.

After I finished reading all the details, he started to walk me through the will. "I advised Rosie to set up the trust before her death to protect it from her family members and to protect you just in case you divorce Darren, or he dies. All her stateside properties were liquidated. You and Winston have joint ownership of the Jamaican property and her trust. Her life insurance and her offshore accounts were placed in the trust. As of closing today, the cash value of the trust is fifteen million dollars."

After he finished with the will, he handed me two envelopes. One read, WHEN YOU ARE AS FREE AS I KNOW YOU CAN BE, and the other contained a lockbox key. He said, "The lockbox has been turned over to you. Just sign the signature card and drop it off at the bank."

Before going home, I stopped by the bank and switched the box to my name. The lady walked me to the vault. I could not bring myself to go through it, so I opened the box just enough to place all the papers and the letter within.

When I got back to the car, I broke down. At that moment, I promised Rosie, "I will sit down with the box when I am free."

When I got home, I needed to just hold the ring that Rosie gave me. Looking through the jewelry box in my closet, I had trouble finding it.

Where in the hell is my ring? No one knows she gave me this ring, so I can't ask Darren. I know he has that ring, but how in the hell did he get into the drawer? Let me think. He bought the cabinet. I bet he had an extra key. I should have known. Thank God, I was smart enough to put the will in a lockbox at the bank.

When I got back to the sofa, I cried out, "Rosie, I am so sorry for letting you down!" I did not have the energy to get up, so I just stayed there until I fell asleep.

When I woke up, my eyes were dry, but my heart was still aching. I jumped into the shower to pull myself together. I stood under the hot, running water with my eyes shut. As I relaxed, my mind moved from the stolen ring to all the good times shared with Rosie. I tell you no lie, out of nowhere an aromatic scent of roses filled the shower.

I held my face back, and I could feel my tears just wash away.

CHAPTER 24

SOUP OF THE DAY

Michael

When I got up this morning, I had this strange craving for seafood soup. Checking the pantry and freezer, I had everything I needed.
So, let's do it. Wait, the only thing missing is Joy and Gypsy. This soup doesn't taste right without sharing.
My phone was at low battery. *I better put my phone on the charger and use my earbuds.*
Sounding chipper, Gypsy answered, "Well, hello, young lady. How are you doing?"
"I'm doing just lovely. Look, I'm making seafood soup. Should be ready in about an hour. I would love for you and Joy to come over for dinner. Please give Joy a call and let her know."
"Now, that sounds yummy. I was just about to call Joy anyway. She'll be there, so count her in. You know she would not miss out on a bowl of your seafood soup."
"Gypsy, one more thing," I said. "Darren is scheduled to be home sometime tomorrow, so you all can take

whatever we have left. You know he's allergic to seafood, so I try not to have any in the refrigerator."

"Not a problem. I'll let Joy know. See you later."

I loved my seafood soup. It made me think of Rosie. She taught me how to make it the last time I was in Jamaica. One of her secrets was not only to boil the shrimp shells, but sauté the shrimp.

After I cooked, I decided to clean the refrigerator out. I couldn't believe all of the take-out containers of half-eaten food Darren had. *Look at this mess.* He had spilled juice and was too lazy to wipe the mess up.

He kills me, acting like he has a house full of people cleaning up after him. You know what? I'm not going to let his trifling butt spoil my evening. Let me listen to something to clear my head. Thank goodness, he won't be back home until tomorrow.

CHAPTER 25

RIGHT BETWEEN THE EYES

Darren

Michael isn't expecting me until tomorrow. I hate going home, but I guess arriving unexpectedly might be a good thing. I could catch her having an affair, file for divorce, and then I could marry Suga. Now, that's wishful thinking. Nobody wants her, not even me.

To be honest, the only reason I hadn't filed for divorce was I knew Michael would clean my clock. The way she was so hooked at the hip with those two skank girlfriends, I'd have to fight all three of them.

When I walked in the house, she had all my food on the damn counter. "Michael, what do you think you're doing?"

Now, I knew damn well she heard me, but she didn't answer. "Michael!"

Boy, she was really pissing me off. First, I didn't want to be here, then she was being slick. I guess she got this cute move from that crazy Joy. "Michael!"

Is this little bitch ignoring me? She just doesn't know she's playing with fire tonight.

Through my rage, the only sight was her skinny butt sticking out of the refrigerator. Before I knew it, I took my foot and kicked her right in the middle of her narrow ass. When she started to scream, I said, "I bet you heard that!"

After she got herself together, she just looked at me like, *Where in the hell did you come from?*

"Do not play with me tonight! You heard me!" I said.

"First of all, I was not expecting you until late tomorrow," she said, "and secondly, I had my earbuds on."

Looking at her, I thought, *Now, she's lying,* even though she took them out of her ears.

"You heard me!" Before I knew it, I slapped that little monkey so hard, she landed on the floor. When she tried to get up, I put my foot on her throat. I told her, "Stay down there until I tell you to get up!"

I left the room and went into the bedroom closet. I took one of those wire hangers and walked over to the hall closet. Standing there, I screamed, "Where is that damn duct tape?"

Before I closed the door, I spotted it under the towels. *So now she's hiding my shit?* I went back into the kitchen. She was on the floor, not saying a word. I wrapped that hanger with duct tape. When I finished, pulling her by the hair, I told her to pull her dress up and roll over.

In the middle of her tears, she said, "Why are you doing this? What is wrong with you?"

I said, "Skank, *you* are what's wrong with me. I hate you. Now, turn over and pull your dress up!"

When I looked down, I could see the river she had cried. I told her, "Save your fake tears. I'm going to give you something to cry about."

I beat her until I was hungry. When I finished, I rolled her over and, looking her right in her eyes, I told her, "Stay there until I tell you to get up."

Standing in front of the fridge, trying to see what I could quickly fix, I noticed my favorite sausages. I closed the door and stepped over her. While cutting up my sausages, I told her if she told them gal friends about this, I was going to break her skinny neck. As soon as I reached for the small frying pan in the sink, this fool started talking.

Before I knew it, I was standing over her with the damn pan. "I told you not to speak!"

Before she could react, I reached down and slapped her right in the mouth. Watching the meat cook, I told her, "If I hear another word, I'm going to pour this hot grease on you. Let me think . . . mustard and mayonnaise . . . or jelly."

Looking in the pantry, I couldn't find jelly, so I guessed it would be mustard and my favorite mayonnaise. I put my sandwich on the plate sitting in the sink. When I picked it up, this skank sat up and called my name. With my sandwich in hand, I walked over to her crying, screaming ass. "Shut up!" Standing over her, I said, "If I have to tell you one more time, I'm going to choke you."

I guess she wanted a piece of my sandwich, because her eyes followed it like she was getting an eye exam. Right as she blinked, a big glob of mustard landed between her eyes.

While I stood over her, I thought of the life-insurance policies we took out after we got married. "My money problems would be over if you would just lie down and die! You are worth more to me dead than alive."

As I pulled my sandwich closer to my mouth, she started to open hers. Before she said a word, I said, "I dare you."

Now that she was quiet, I got back to my sandwich. Before I finished, I started to itch, and my hands started to swell. Struggling to breathe, my throat tightened, and the room got dark.

CHAPTER 26

BTWHWYWACYACC

Joy

Gypsy called me to let me know she was going to pick me up at three. To be honest, I forgot that Michael invited us over before Shithead came back from down south.
I don't give a damn. I know that was him at the mall.
But I was going to go with Gypsy and not trust my eyes. I guess I needed to schedule an eye appointment before I get somebody killed.

Before I left, I knew I should let the dogs out. "Who has to pot-pot?" As soon as I said that, both beat me to the door. "Wait, Maxx. Maxx!"

I left the gate open on the porch, and there he went, running after the deer. Dammit, the only thing I had on was an oversize tee, no undies, and no shoes—and no, I did not want to run in the freaking mud. I needed to catch him before he headed for the woods.

When we reached our yard, holding the leash tightly in my hand, I pushed him down. I told him, "If this happens again, I'm taking my time coming to get you." He started to run for the patio. "Hell no, buddy. Neither you nor I are going into the house covered in mud."

So, I dragged him under the patio with me to retrieve the water hose. *Damn, this water is cold.*

After we finished, we ran up the patio stairs. "Sweetie, you are going to stay out here until you dry off."

After locking the gate, I walked back into the house. Now, what got me the most was when Maxx stared at me like, *Heifer, I know I'm going to get a treat.* I just looked at him and walked away. Before I could turn, he started barking and running in circles. By this time, I was wet, tired, and scratched up, and the last thing I needed was to hear his mouth, so I gave him a cat treat.

I jumped in the shower, and as soon as I got in, the damn phone went off. By the ringtone, I knew it was Gypsy.

I tried to reach the phone without getting out of the shower, but I couldn't. I did what a girl had to do: I took my back scrubber and pushed the phone closer. Just as I reached my phone, she hung up. *She can wait. Just my luck, I'll drop my phone in the tub.*

When I got out of the shower, I called her back, but she didn't answer.

Gypsy called back, sounding a little worried. "Turn that damn music down. I was calling to see if you were getting ready."

Knowing this would piss her off, I said, "Yes, ma'am, I is." And I turned the music down.

"You should have enough speaking like that. One day you're going to slip at the wrong time and look like a straight-up fool," she said. "Anyway, I called Michael to see if she needs us to pick up anything, but she didn't answer. I'll try again later. Just be ready."

Shortly after, the dogs started raising hell, so I knew someone was in the driveway. Pulling back the curtains, I saw that it was Gypsy. "Look, guys, be good. Do not pee in the house, and I love you."

When I got in the car, I asked if Michael needed anything. Sounding a little concerned, she said, "She's still not picking up."

About a mile from Michael's, Gypsy tried calling again. No answer. I told her, "I bet she's in the shower. If she needs something, she'll send you out for it."

When we reached the house, Darren's car was parked in the grass. Looking at Gypsy, I said, "I thought you said Darren wouldn't be back until tomorrow. See, that boy-bitch is home."

I picked up Gypsy's phone and redialed Michael. Again, no answer.

Placing the phone in my lap, I said to Gypsy, "Girl, look how Darren's car is parked. It not even resting on the driveway. I really think something's going on. You know a lot of his clients are just as shady as he is. Maybe he lost someone's case, and they're seeking revenge."

Looking at me and not smiling, Gypsy said, "Joy, where in the hell do you get these crazy assumptions? They are probably hanging out by the pool."

"Wait, you are talking about *my* assumptions? I tell you what, Ms. Gypsy. How about you get out the damn car and go ring the doorbell?"

"Fine. I can do that. You are taking this situation way too far."

While Gypsy rang the doorbell, I continued to call. No one answered the door or phone. I started to get nervous when Gypsy called me and told me to look under the driver's seat for her gun and bring her car keys.

When I handed her the gun, she told me to use Michael's key and unlock the door.

I put the key in the lock and turned it. Stepping back, I said, "Look, you know damn well Darren does not like me. I'm not giving him an opportunity to shoot me. How about you open the door and walk the hell in? Wait, before you do that, let me check to see if the gate is open. If it is, I think we should check to see if they're out back before we go into the house."

Walking over to the gate, I didn't hear anyone moving around or talking. When I tried to open the gate, it was locked.

Going back to the front door, I told Gypsy, "The gate's locked, and it doesn't sound like anyone's in the backyard."

"Okay, let's go in," Gypsy said, "but you're going in first."

At the same time, we placed one foot in the house. "Hello?" Then the second foot. "Hello?"

No answer. Following Gypsy, I pulled out the knife I kept in my bra. I'm sure we looked like Dorothy when they were getting ready to pull back the curtain on the Wizard.

We stood at the bottom of the stairs leading to the second level.

"Michael? Darren?"

No answer.

When we reached the family area, we could hear the TV blaring, but still no sign of anyone.

By this time, we both agreed something was not right and we should call the police. "Gypsy, before you call, why don't you look inside the cars?"

"Good idea." Handing me the gun, she told me to stand at the door until she got back.

I waited until she turned and walked toward the cars, then I went back into the house. This time I went back down the gray hallway and through the family room toward the kitchen.

When I walked into the kitchen, I almost shot my foot.

Both Michael and Darren were on the floor. Now, get this: Darren was lying almost on top of Michael. With my back away from the door, I walked over and placed the gun and knife on the counter. Leaning down, I rolled Darren off Michael as much as I could. In the process, I "accidentally" stepped on him.

When I was able to get to Michael, I jumped back. I saw mustard right in the middle of her forehead, the bruises on her face, and her lip bloody and swollen. "Baby girl, baby girl, are you okay?"

She tried to answer, but she could barely open her mouth.

I pulled out my phone and called 911. "Look, just stay lying down until I get back." When I stood up, I "accidentally" stepped on Darren's head.

I started running for the front door. When I got to the living room, Gypsy was running toward me. "I thought I told you to stay at the door!"

She could tell something was not right with me, and I just turned and ran back to the kitchen, not saying another word. Gypsy started running behind me. When we reached the kitchen, Gypsy looked like she was going into shock.

Darren did not move through the entire process.

"Not sure what's wrong with him, but his face and lips are extremely swollen."

"Damn, I wonder if Michael jacked him up."

Hearing the sirens, Gypsy told me to stay with Michael

while she met the paramedics. I hid Gypsy's gun and my knife under the sofa in the den. After Gypsy left, Michael just moaned and cried.

Before the emergency folk arrived, I stood over Darren. For a moment, I had flashes of some of his low-down shit. I guess I got caught up in my emotions because I screamed, "Boy, this what happens when you write a check yo' ass can't cash."

Gypsy came back with a tall lady officer. When she saw the situation, she unclipped her gun holder before checking on Michael. "Ma'am, are you okay?"

Michael didn't say a word.

Without taking her eyes off Michael, the lady cop started questioning Gypsy and me. While I tried to explain what we found, the cop told Gypsy to go wait at the front door for the paramedics.

Gypsy came back with help in tow. One guy checked on Michael, and the other checked on Darren. To me, he looked dead. Now, *that* could have been wishful thinking.

Stop, Joy!

The paramedics helped Michael onto the gurney and rolled her out to the ambulance. Gypsy and I were right behind her when they loaded her in. Gypsy jumped in her car and followed the ambulance to the hospital.

I stood in the doorway, numb, confused, hurt, and just pissed. *God, why sweet Michael?*

I went back to the kitchen. Darren was still on the floor. The police told me Darren was dead, and they had to wait on the coroner before they could move him. The lady cop asked me not to leave, because she needed my help with her report and wanted me to secure the house.

Sitting on the living-room sofa, the lady cop said, "Ma'am, I know you're upset, but keep in mind that this is an active investigation. Now, explain how you all got into the house."

"We're her best friends. We have keys to each other's homes. When no one answered, we decided to do a wellness check."

The policewoman shared that she walked around the lower part of the house and didn't see any sign of forced entry. When we wrapped up, she and I walked through the house again to see if I noticed anything. When we were done, I grabbed Michael's car keys from the table next to the front door and locked up.

On my way to Michael's car, she said for me to follow her to the hospital.

When I got to the hospital, I didn't see Gypsy, but the paramedics were still there. They told me she was in the back. The medical examiner told us Darren had white powder in his nostrils, which could be cocaine, but he died from some type of allergic reaction.

Damn, Michael, you sly fox, you killed him with shrimp!

After Michael came around, she said, "I tried to tell him not to use the pan because I had cooked the shrimp in it, but he kept hitting me and telling me to shut my damn mouth."

When Gypsy and I left the room, I whispered, "Who would ever thunk shrimp was the best medicine for your headache and heart pain? You can't make this crazy up if you tried."

CHAPTER 27

MY EYES DON'T LIE

Joy

On the day of Darren's service, Gypsy and I helped Michael dress. Poor Michael's face was bruised and swollen. To hide her injuries, Michael had to wear a veil and dark shades.

The only reason I was there was to support Michael. She should have had him cremated, then flushed his evil, cheating, lying, woman-beating, coke-sniffing, trick ass down the toilet at a gas station.

I noticed the procession of people viewing the body and giving their condolences to Michael, one tall lady that seemed to be grieving harder than Michael caught my eye. As she got closer, I kept asking myself, *Where do I know this sea hag from?*

While she waited to view the body, I got a good look at her, and then I remembered. *What the total fuck? That's that trick I saw at the mall in Jacksonville!*

After she viewed the body, this hag turned in Michael's

direction, but in the middle of her stride, she looked straight at me. I guess the way I was looking at her made her stop, because she stepped out of the procession and went back to her seat.

Near the end of the service, I had to run to the restroom. Guess who was coming out as I was walking in? That's right, little Miss Crying-Sea-Hag. Before I knew it, I grabbed her arm and pulled her right back in.

"Hey, heifer, were you in Jacksonville a couple of weeks ago?"

Sounding nervous, she replied, "Yes, how did you know? And who are you?"

"Look, trick, you do not need to know who I am. I know why you're here. When I let you out of this restroom, go get your shit and haul ass, and I better not see your skank ass at the gravesite."

Trying to act like she had some balls, she said, "Lady, you're crazy. Leave me alone."

Lord, help me. Before I knew it, I pulled her to the sink and pushed her face against the mirror. I told her, "Look, honey, I am not going to stand for you disrespecting my girl by being here."

When she placed her hand on the mirror, my eyes zoomed in on the ring that she was wearing.

Damn real, my eyes did not lie to me.

Sitting on her freshly manicured fingers was Michael's ring. Before I knew it, I pulled my knife out of my bra, and I told her, "Give me that damn ring."

Instead of giving me the ring, she had the nerve to say, "I can't believe I'm being robbed in a church."

With a slow whisper, I said, "Look, that ring belongs to my girl, not you. It's her grandmother's. Now, I need to go watch them throw ya dick in a hole, so hurry the hell up, and don't think for one second you are going to cross that threshold with Michael's ring in your ass pocket."

When I said that, she fell to the floor crying like a baby. The more she cried, the deeper her voice got. The more she wiped her face, the less made-up she looked. Looking at her long, crusty feet made me want to throw the hell up. Leaning down for a closer look, the only words I was able to say were, "Trick, please tell me you are not a boy."

Holding her hands over her face, she replied, "Not really. I'm in transition."

"Hold up," I said. "I know that trick upstairs in the casket has transitioned to hell, but where are *you* going?"

Sitting up, she replied, "I was scheduled for sex-reassignment surgery before Darren died. He planned on leaving his wife and marrying me after my surgery."

"What? Give me my friend's freaking ring and transition your ass out of this church *now*."

After she gave me the ring, she had the damn nerve to ask me to help her up. Instead of responding, I walked over to the sink, washed Michael's ring off, placed it in my purse, put my knife back in my bra, and walked out of the restroom. "Lord forgive me for cursing and fighting in church. Amen."

By the time I made it back upstairs, they were loading him in the hearse. Gypsy came over and whispered, "Where the hell have you been?"

Looking straight ahead, I said, "Girl, I got something hot to tell you, but not now."

At the gravesite, Michael's friend Winston hung around in the background. After the internment, he escorted her to the waiting limo and left with her.

Walking to the car, Gypsy started to give me a lecture

about leaving the service. When we reached the car, I handed her my purse and told her to look inside and open the wet paper towel.

When she opened it, she said, "Isn't this the ring Michael thought she lost?"

"Yep." Then I took her step by step on how I recovered it and told her, "When you get a chance, place it deep down in the jewelry box that she has on her dresser. One day she'll find it. Gypsy, you know, this boy-girlfriend situation explains it all."

Rolling her eyes, Gypsy asked, "Explain what? He's an abuser, a liar, and a thief."

"No, Darren's disrespect of women. Think about it. He constantly referred to women as bitches, hoes, and skanks. Can you recall him saying anything pleasant about a woman? Let Michael tell it, intimacy was for just making a baby, so he could cash in on inheritance from Tee, his mom's mother. Hell, they probably thought hanging money over his head would keep him in the closet. It explains why innocent Michael was such a good 'catch.' It explains why Rosie—his dad's mother—was so close and protective of Michael. I bet Rosie is dancing in heaven as we speak.

"Lord knows I am not making excuses for him, but to be honest, he was rotten, frustrated, and scared to come out of the closet. Dealing with a transsexual was safe. Lord, I hate to say this, but I am glad it ended this way. This mess would have destroyed poor Michael."

Voice breaking, Gypsy added, "Not to mention the way he belittled and beat that sweet girl was just horrible. The sad thing? She fought so hard for her marriage. Girl, we need to make sure Michael never finds out about the ring and the boyfriend."

With tear-filled eyes, I agreed. "Gypsy, see? When you live a lie, everybody suffers. Live in your truth and let others live in theirs."

Gypsy shouted, "Turn around and go back to the graveyard!"

Looking at her like she'd lost her mind, I said, "For what?"

"So I can dig him up and cut his head off. Girl, you know you cannot make this madness up."

I laughed so hard, I jerked the wheel.

After getting to Michael's house, we walked into the house to see Winston and Michael sitting on the sofa, kind of close. I grabbed my phone and texted Gypsy, WELL DAMN.

CHAPTER 28

COMMUNICATION

Joy

On my way upstairs, I heard my phone. When I answered, L was on the other end. He asked, "How is *my* sweet Candy Cane?"

Smiling inside, I said, "Your Candy is doing awesome, now that I'm talking to you."

"Awesome. Baby, I've been thinking about what our relationship needs to grow, and what comes to mind is open communication, trust, and no walls. I can't speak for you, but for me, my past life has made me live in silence behind a wall of mistrust. I'm a work in progress, but I'm committed to growing our relationship. All I am asking from you it to trust and communicate with me like you did when you were sixteen, and allow me to tear down any walls life has built. Your thoughts?"

"Damn, L, after all these years, we still think alike," I said. "I agree. Communication is key, but for me, trust trumps all. My current level of trust is light years away from my sixteen-year-old self. Over the years, life has forced me to lock my heart behind a wall of fear. I am committed, but I need you to be patient with me as we grow together."

"Candy, I understand, but will you let me go beyond not just your walls? I need to come inside, remove all your trap doors, find all your hiding places, and then I need to tear down your safe place. Until this is done, we aren't communicating how we should be. We're just talking," he said. "Baby, your past has nothing to do with where we are at this moment. However, your past can and will impact how we move forward if you don't surrender. Baby, do you agree?"

Thinking about how safe I felt the last time I surrendered to him, in a low whisper I said, "I do."

"My sweet Candy, thank you." Then he said, "Close your eyes and let me visit your imagination. Stop your mind from spinning, take a deep breath, and look at that lovely lady standing in front of you. She's the empress I want us to meet. Let me make this clear: I'm not perfect, and there is nothing wrong with you. I just know there is a better you and me ready to step up and out. Baby, I would like to talk to you every day. Are you good with that?"

With my eyes still closed, all I could say was, "I would love that."

"Candy, God has been good to me. I have a life that some people only dream about. All the material things that I have collected over the years mean nothing without you in my life. Look, I'm totally free. I don't have a baby mama. I don't have a string of women. The only thing that I have is my love for you. I never let you go, and I will never let you go."

Then, in that sweet voice of his, L said, "Before I called

you, I listened to my favorite Bloodstone song, 'Never Let You Go.' I don't know if you remember, but that was one of the songs playing when I carried you over to womanhood. Candy, trust me, nothing has changed. I never let you go, and I will never let us go. I love you. Hear me, baby. I love you."

Feeling warm inside, I said, "I'm listening to you, and I hear the same L I knew when I was sixteen. God knows I never stopped loving you. All I ask is for you to be patient with me."

Laughing, he said, "I am as patient as I was when you were sixteen. Candy, I'm sorry for talking your ear off. Before I hang up, I want to leave you with my favorite Bob Marley quote, 'The biggest coward is a man who awakens a woman's love with no intention of loving her.' Baby, I'm not a coward, and I have loving intentions for you and for us.

"Candy, I'm in therapy, I want you to consider doing the same. We left each other broken. I never married. You married multiple times—seems like I'm waiting and you're searching for love. I know this isn't normal. My therapist told me I locked my heart when we departed, and the only person that has the key is you. Have a good night, and I will talk to you tomorrow. Love you, baby."

"L, that is what I wanted to hear. By the way, I am in therapy for other issues. But I am sure we will get to my emotional walls. Love you. Good night."

CHAPTER 29

ALWAYS FIND TIME TO LAUGH

Joy

I just *had* to call Gypsy to give her a good laugh. With all that was going on, shit, we both needed a little laughter.

"Gypsy, I got something funny to tell you. Can you talk?"

"Sure, I'm home," she said. "My day has been crazy. The way you sound, I know this is going to be off the chain."

"Gypsy, check this out. I am sitting in the waiting room at Dr. Sheeley's office, thumbing through a magazine. Suddenly, the office door flies open, and a man stepped in, looking like Rambo. He walked up to the counter and just stood there. This stand was not the stand you take when you're waiting on the receptionist to get off the phone. It was more like, *Woman, get off the phone.*

When she looked up, I heard her ask him, 'May I help you?' Killer Rambo didn't open his mouth, and she asked again. Again, he did not open his mouth. I heard her rolling chair slide back, then I saw her standing up. With the sound of concern in her voice, she asked, 'Sir, are you all right?' Now, I was praying he would answer, but he said nothing."

Like she feared the answer, Gypsy said, "Joy, what did you do?"

I said, "What the hell did you think I did? I got up and moved by the exit door. I knew the alarm would go off, so I just stood in front of it. And I thought, *This is a shrink's office. I am the only Black person in the waiting room, and I am the only person at the emergency door.* But I didn't give a hoot. I wasn't going to be on the inside of the yellow tape.

"I could see the nurse standing behind the receptionist, and like toy soldiers in *The Nutcracker*, both started to step back. From where I was sitting, I could see their eyes looking toward the door to the hallway. The damn office phone started ringing. Now, what concerned me was they just let it ring. No one dared to go back to the front desk. And by this time the lady that was across from me in the waiting room was standing in front of me at the emergency exit."

"What happened?" Gypsy asked.

I said, "Well, I'm not sure what triggered him, but he stood back on his right leg and reached into his shoulder bag and pulled out this big binder. In a loud voice, he said, 'Is this the unemployment office?'"

Gypsy laughed. "The unemployment office? You can't make that story up if you tried."

"Girl, correct, I couldn't. They told him it wasn't, and he picked up the binder and just left. I didn't leave the exit door until I saw him cross the threshold. After I heard the door click, I walked up to the counter and asked if I could use the restroom. Then I thought, *Forget therapy. I need a drink.* Girl, I told the receptionist I needed to reschedule, and I left."

Gypsy asked, "Why does dumb crap always happen to you? I needed that laugh. Girl, stop by so I can fix you a real strong drink."

I screamed, "Girl, I am on my way."

CHAPTER 30

THE DUSTY ROAD HOME

Gypsy

I jumped in my car as soon as the guys finished opening the farm gate entrance and followed them down Dry Lake Road. As I've gotten older, I appreciate the dust flying in the air, the washboard roads, and the honeysuckles hanging from the fence. At the four-way stop, I kept straight until I reached the old, abandoned, wooden school my dad attended. Turning off the road, I circled the old oak tree, then I turned right back onto Dry Lake Road and headed home.

After I turned on the road leading to the farm, I stopped at the family graveyard, marveling at how my family has kept up the grounds. From the headstones, my family has been here for over two hundred years. The story goes that Big Mama's daddy, Sammuel produced twelve children, six White and six Black. Get this: each set of kids were the same age, with the same name. I have a White Uncle

Sammy and a Black Uncle Sammy, both eighty-six. I guess segregation kept down the confusion in those days.

Big Mama's daddy was a man way ahead of his time, a free thinker. He said that things were going to change, and that, in time, the world would wake up, but until then he was going to stay woke. Every night, he would drive down to have dinner or dessert with his Black family, and he made sure all his kids played together.

He said, "I'm not going to have any of my kids not knowing their people." It broke him up when his Black kids had to call him Mr. Sam, but he made them do it because he did not want them to slip in public.

He was buried in the center of this graveyard with all his descendants around him. He used to say, "I did not separate them in life. Why would I do it in death?"

Before leaving, I stood at the entrance and screamed out, "I love you all. Thanks for paving the way to my dreams."

After praying, I moved toward the entrance to the gravesite to head home. I noticed a cloud of dust heading my way, then slow down and turn into the farm. Standing with my hand blocking the sun, I noticed one car was the local sheriff and the other car I didn't know. When they turned in, I stepped in the middle of the road for them to stop.

Sheriff Hunter and I embraced when he got out of the car. Afterward, he introduced the men in the other cars as the agents from the Georgia Bureau of Investigation and the FBI.

A little perplexed, I asked, "So, what brings you guys out?"

"We are here concerning what happened with Aunt Betty," said Sheriff Hunter. "I'm glad we found her, but I wanted to let you know I won't be working on your case anymore. Charles is going to be charged with elder abuse, and since he took her over state lines, the FBI will take over your case, and the GBI will handle the elder-abuse charges."

Still pissed, I said, "Good. He needs to be stopped. Treating his mother like that is so tragic—for him and her. Do me a favor. Don't go up to the house. If Aunt Betty found out about the charges, she would be devastated. A mother's love is strange. In her mind, he's still her baby. In my eyes, he's a criminal."

Both the FBI and the GBI agents introduced themselves to me. I told them, "I have guardianship over my aunt, so I'll be your point of contact. Please don't share any information with anyone else." I pulled out my phone and told them, "I installed security cameras in Aunt Betty's house. If Charles shows back up, you'll be the first people I call."

We exchanged contact information. Looking back at the house, I saw Big Daddy stepping off the porch. "Guys, if he comes out here, please don't mention anything about the charges against Charles. Just tell him you all were leaving town and wanted to stop by."

When I turned back around, I noticed Big Daddy walking toward the henhouse.

When the agents left, Sheriff Hunter said, "Gypsy, if you're finished up here, I'll follow you up to the house. I know Big Mama. She's making homemade biscuits, and you know I gotta get some."

We drove slowly back to the farm, taking in the beauty of the land. At the end of the road, Sheriff Hunter pulled up to the porch as I stopped before driving under the gate I just installed. It said, "Welcome to the Family Farm," and above that was a banner that said, "Grand Opening." I loved the fact the welder was able to use the old gate. I thanked God for this gift, then I asked Him to continue to guide my steps.

After I parked, I stood at the entrance to the residential area. The cafeteria, recreation area, homes, and community garden made the farm look like a small village. Big Daddy had recommended the community garden. He'd said, "The children should have hands-on farming experience in a controlled environment, and it'll give the residents something to keep them busy."

It made me feel so proud to offer a place where the old and the young could spend quality time together, where they could bond, and where the kids could just be kids, just like what I had when I was a kid. I was very fortunate to be able to hire good staff, teachers, nurses, and professionals to manage the cafeteria.

On my way back to the main house, one of my cousins walked up with building materials. I stopped him and asked what he was up to.

"Girl, Big Mama had me come down and build a chicken pen."

Laughing at the expression on his face, all I could say was, "What the hell?"

"Yep, you know she wasn't going to let Big Daddy have the ups on her with the community garden, so she had me come down and set up a coop so the kids would know about taking care of the chickens and collecting eggs. Now, you know damn well who's going to be the one to have to keep it clean."

I expected him to say it would be him, but instead, he said, "You are."

When I got back to the main house, seeing all the old heads drinking coffee, cooking, and talking trash took me on a natural high. Today's activities and having me around had really blown a breath of fresh air into their lungs.

Looking at all my blood family, I started to really miss my love family. I asked Michael, Joy, and the crowd to come down, but unfortunately, everyone had plans. I promised them I would send pictures. *I guess it's a simple substitute.*

Let me get out of my head. I need to run to town to pick up the T-shirts.

Before I left, I opened the screen door and yelled, "I'm going to town. Do I need to pick up anything?"

Granny and Big Mama yelled, "Child, no."

Before I reached the car, Aunt Betty came running down the stairs screaming a list of items I needed to pick up for her. Taking in her smile and beauty in the sunlight, I said, "Girlfriend, you know I can't remember all that. Get your pretty self in the car, and let's go."

The expression on her face took me back to when I was a little girl running around with her.

Aunt Betty and I ran around town all day. On the way home, it broke my heart when she looked at me and asked, "Baby, can we ride by my house before heading to the farm?"

Trying not to cry, I told her, "Well, not until we stop for some ice cream." When I said that, all she did was smile.

After picking up ice cream, I thought about how, when I was pregnant, she would bring me a big pint of ice cream at least once a week.

When I turned down her street, my heart started racing. *What if she wants to stop and that fucking Charles is in the house?* So, I told her, "Girlfriend, you know Big Mama is waiting on us, so we can't stop now."

Eating her ice cream, she said, "You're right, baby. Let's just drive by."

"Girl, get out of that ice cream cup and look at your house," I said as we got closer.

"I will," she smiled.

Damn, I am all jacked up. Jesus, take the wheel.

When we got back to the farm, I jokingly said to Aunt Betty, "Girlfriend, we better hide our trash. Big Mama'll be pissed if she knew we were eating right before dinner."

When we walked into the house, Granny and Big Mama were cleaning the kitchen. Looking at both of us, Big Mama said, "Nothing changes. I can remember you running around with Betty and missing dinner."

Granny chimed in, "Yep. I bet they had ice cream."

After dinner, Granny went upstairs to help Aunt Betty get ready for bed. I sat out on the front-porch swing, and Big Mama came out with a tray of cookies and milk. I stopped the swing so she could join me. We made small talk while we enjoyed our cookies.

Listening to the crickets and swinging, I broke the silence. "Big Mama, when I was pregnant, I would come out here after you all went to bed, and for the hell of me, you would always find me."

Smiling, she said, "Yes, baby, I kept—we all kept—our eyes on you. Baby, when you hurt, we all hurt. Remember, I told you to just trust in God, and it'll all work out. Now, look at the twins. Doctors saving lives and giving love. See? God does not make mistakes."

Laying my head on her soft shoulders, I told her, "Thank you for supporting and believing in me."

Patting my knee, she said, "Baby, you are welcome. Thank you for trusting us."

Suddenly, Granny came out with another tray of

cookies and milk. I scooted over for her to join us. Sitting in the middle of these two angels, eating my second round of cookies, I felt loved and safe.

All the coming and going woke me up. I jumped up to get ready for the big day. The aroma of love permeating from the kitchen put a little pep in my step.

When I got to the bottom of the stairs, I stopped to greet the lady looking at me, feeling excited, but missing my girls. I understood that they had plans, and I was sure they would be down before the end of the summer.

Standing at the kitchen door, I wanted to cry. My aunts, uncles, and cousins were moving around wearing the family farm T-shirts I'd bought.

"Morning, family."

I turned on the radio, and the song "Do the Bump" came on. The twins broke out with a happy dance, and not to be outdone, Aunt Betty joined in.

People from all the surrounding towns were pulling up. As far as you could see down that dusty road were trucks, cars, and even a wagon. Big Mama called me in to help her bring out her homemade cookies and cakes.

Stepping into the kitchen, I heard Big Mama ending her call with, "Okay, baby."

With a large tray of desserts, I turned my back to open the screen door, but before I reached the bottom stair, my uncle took the tray and said, "Girl, go greet your guests. I got this."

Standing in the front yard, I noticed the road dust flying like a helicopter was landing. In the middle of the dust were two RVs. I watched them make their way up the drive, and when it got closer, I saw two familiar faces: TJ looking straight ahead and Maxx peeking from behind.

Before I knew it, I was running down the drive. Before I got to the RV parking area, my Atlanta family jumped out: Joy, Michael, Winston, Gus, and some of Michael's catering crew. All of them started running toward me, and when we connected, we started spinning each other around. It warmed my heart to see everyone, including TJ and Maxx, wearing white bandannas around their necks.

With tears flowing, I said, "I thought you all weren't coming!"

Michael hugged me. "You know damn well we weren't going to miss your day. You win, we win. You celebrate, we celebrate. You cry, we cry."

We all held hands as we walked up to the gate. Suddenly, I heard Joy scream, "Oh, hell no!"

Just like in the past, TJ and Maxx ran ahead of us then stopped right in front of us, and when we tried to go around, TJ started to growl. What did we do? We fell in formation: TJ leading, Maxx taking up the rear, us fools in the middle, and the last person screaming, "Maxx, stop jumping on my legs!"

Later, another bus pulled up, and all of us went down to greet the guests. To my surprise, these were the new residents and their grandkids. I personally escorted each resident to their new home, and Joy and Michael led the kids to their housing.

During the cafeteria tour, I noticed two ladies in the kitchen: Velma and Wilma from Michael's catering business. I ran and gave them a big, old hug. I asked, "Why are you all in here?"

Still holding my hand, Velma said, "We're on the kitchen staff." I must have been looking puzzled, because she went on, "Baby, Michael got us the jobs here. We moved down last week. We kept out of sight until today."

Holding both, I said, "I am so glad you all are here. Welcome."

Dottie, another of Michael's former employees, came out. "I thank Michael for referring them. They're the best!"

Velma said, "Baby, we need to get back to work, but stop by the house after the dust settles."

Dottie shared, "The resident count, as of today, is fifteen permanent residents and twenty kids for the entire summer." When she finished with the update, she reached over to close my mouth. "Gypsy, we wanted to surprise you. Let's get together in the morning to go over the summer-camp details."

Walking around the farm, it was so fulfilling to see the kids enjoying their grandparents and the seniors enjoying each other, all one big family. Just how I envisioned it.

Later in the month, I went to the bank to make my first payment. While I was sitting in the waiting area, this tall, blond, good ol' boy greeted me, and with that southern drawl, he introduced himself as Chris Henry, then he asked me to come to his office.

When I sat down, Chris shared, "I really enjoyed the grand opening, and the town needs your services. What are you in for today?"

"Nothing much. I'm coming in to pay my first mortgage payment."

Smiling, he opened the folder on his desk. "Ms. Gypsy, I won't be able to help you with your payment."

Sitting back in my chair, I said, "No worries. I can give it to the teller."

While I was talking, he handed me the envelope that he took out of the folder. After reading it, I told him, "There must be some kind of mistake."

Then Chris handed me the deed to the farm and a note. "No mistake, Ms. Gypsy."

Reading the note, tears ran down my cheeks. Reaching over to get a tissue, Chris asked, "Are you okay?"

Instead of answering, I shared the note. It said, "Thanks for everything. Nothing like being free. Love, Michael."

I saw the banker looking out of the window. When he turned, you could see that he was touched. Chris shared, "My mother's in good health, very independent, and I would like for her to be closer to me. Could you—?"

I told him, "We would love to have her." I gave him Dottie's contact info.

Reaching for it, he said, "She'll be down in a month." Then, smiling, Chris said, "Not sure if you know it, but we're related."

"What is the connection?" I asked.

Smiling, he said, "Our great-granddaddy. Ask Big Mama. Gypsy, your vision for the farm is so enlightening. At the grand opening, I visited our family burial site. 'Elevate your imagination' was engraved on a late-1800s headstone."

I said, "Our ancestors were ahead of their time. They refused to go along just to get along. They were freethinkers, free spirits, and they dared to be original."

CHAPTER 31

LOVE CONNECTION

Joy

Karen was devasted because she hadn't heard from Darren. Bless her heart, she thought she did something to run him off. Lord knows that's so far from the truth.

Thanks a lot, lying Darren. Not only do I have to tell Karen you lied to her, but I also have to tell her you're dead.

It broke my heart to see her keeping hope alive for something that would never happen. I really wanted to get right in her face and scream, "Girl, you got played!" But with her current state of mind, I was sure that would send her over the edge.

Her situation proved my philosophy about relationships. A girl needs to have a pair and a spare, just like driving. It's a terrible spot to be in if you get a flat tire in the middle of the night and don't have a spare tire. Then you drive off and get another flat.

Girl, stop.

Now, if it were me, I would have exposed his

shenanigans from day one, walked away, and never looked back, but I guess a lonely heart is blind.

Girl, think. What would I do? Clear your head, lie down, and smoke some weed. I knew that would help me come up with a plan.

Wait, hold up. I know! I can find her a new man! By the time she fell in love again, she would have forgotten all about Darren's lying, cheating butt. Then I could stop having to hold her hand.

Okay, let me check my contact list. I'm sure I can find her some new loving. Where the hell is my phone? I know I had it this morning when I talked to Gypsy. I need to stop smoking weed. I can't remember a damn thing. I hate to get up, but let me check upstairs . . . not upstairs . . . forget it. I'll let it find me. I need to lie down. I am doing way too much.

Just as I was about to fall asleep, I heard the horn ringtone on my phone: Gus. Sitting up, the sound led me to the table next to me. The phone was on the charger.

Well, damn. Now I know I need to stop smoking. I'm getting stupid.

"Well, good morning, brother Gus."

Sounding a little down, he said, "Hi, baby girl. What are you up to?"

"Hold up. Forget me. How are *you* doing?"

Laughing, he said, "I know who to call when I'm feeling this way."

"Gus, baby, what's wrong?"

"I'm feeling really lonely," he said. "Mama is gone, and I am so used to taking care of her. My aunt wants me to take care of her, but I can't. Now I'm at the point in my life where I need to take care of me."

What he said broke my heart, but it was a good segue into my plan. Trying not to sound like I knew where this was going, I said, "And you are doing a great job of taking care of you. Losing weight and focusing on your health are major and the most important steps."

"You're right, but I feel so emotionally lost. I guess part of my dedication to my mom was me not having to deal with my low self-esteem. I want to find someone that I can give healthy love to."

"Gus," I said, "help me understand. What do you mean by healthy love?"

"Healthy love, meaning loving someone and loving me in the process."

Smiling, I replied, "Got it. Gus, you're a good man. I know there's a special lady for you in this crazy, beautiful world. I know you shared you were doing online dating. How is that going for you?"

"I've met some really nice ladies, but I'm not connecting with them."

"So, do you know why you're not connecting?"

He said, "I think a lot of ladies are still carrying baggage and they think that I'm up to something. Seems like I'm too nice, and they back away."

Trying not to sound overexcited that online dating wasn't working out, I asked him, "Do you remember meeting my boss, Karen, at my promotion party?"

"Yes, I do. Why do you ask?" he replied.

"She is such a lovely person looking for love in all the wrong places. She's ended up getting mistreated. You know what I love about her? She keeps hope alive. Gus, I'm cooking dinner for Gypsy tomorrow. Are you available to join us?"

"Sure. Now I know you, Joy. What are you up to?" he asked.

"Look, I am going to see if Karen can join us. I am going

to leave it at that. You're on your own from there," I said. "Let me ping her, and I'll call you back."

I heard the smile in his voice when he said, "That's a plan."

He was so kind, loving, and looking to settle down now that his mama had died. *This connection just might work out. Now, let me try to drag Karen out of her funk.*

She answered on the second ring. "Now, that's a good sound."

"Hello, Karen. What are you doing?"

"Hello, lady. Just relaxing and watching *The Wiz*," she answered.

She sounded like she was pulling through. Glad she wasn't crying about Darren, I asked, "Are you open for dinner tomorrow?"

She replied, "Yes, I am. I need to get out of this house and get back to living."

"Now, that's my girl. Look, Karen, I'm going to tell you what's up." Trying not to bring up Darren, I said, "I'm not sure if you remember me introducing you to my friend Gus at my promotion party."

"Yes, I remember."

Lord, forgive me for lying. "We talked this morning, and he asked about you," I said.

Her reply made me think I was making progress. "Wow, he remembered me and asked about me?"

"Yes, lady. I told you that you have that magic. Look, he is going to join us. He's a good man, so I want you to open up and let him know you."

I heard her smile when she said, "I'm looking forward to moving on. Thanks for thinking of me."

"Karen, just come. You won't regret it, so see you tomorrow."

Lord knows I needed that short nap. All I need now is a hot cup of afternoon coffee. Waiting on the coffee to brew, the thought of Karen and Gus connecting made me feel good inside.

In the middle of my thoughts, my phone rang. From the ringtone, I knew it was Gypsy.

"Hi, lady, what are you up to?" she said.

Between sips of coffee, I replied, "Just waking up. Funny, I was thinking about giving you a call. What are you up to?"

Gypsy said, "The reason why I'm calling is I just spoke to Michael, and she said she was on her way over with some food from her catering event and told me to call you to come over."

Thinking, *Perfect timing*, I said, "Now that sounds like a yummy offer. I'll be over in an hour. Before I come over, I need to share something with you. Do you have a minute? Karen is down about Darren, a.k.a. Mike. She thinks he just dropped her. She never put it together he was a fake, so I'm going to introduce her to Gus. The catch is, I'm going to have to tell Michael about what he did. Do you mind me bringing it up?"

Slow to answer, Gypsy replied, "You know, Michael knew how low Darren was, so I don't think she would give a hoot."

Agreeing, I said, "I must say, since his passing, she seems to be more relaxed. I'll be over in about an hour. Do you need for me to pick up anything?"

Pausing, Gypsy replied, "I just picked up a bottle of whiskey and Michael made some of her 'special cookies.'"

Laughing, I replied, "I'll bring some smoke. I think we are going to need it. I'll see you in about an hour."

After talking to Gypsy, I thought that being her girls,

maybe we should have told Michael about Darren's little trick earlier, but I learned early in life not to get in the middle of married people's P&D (pussy and dick). But now that he's gone, she should know how low he'd been. She had been with him since college. I was quite sure she had her own Darren horror stories.

I was glad things ended for her the way that they did, but that marriage was an accident waiting to happen. You get back what you put out, and Lord knows Darren had put out a lot of bad energy.

CHAPTER 32

LET HAPPY FIND YOU

Joy

Before leaving the house, I dropped TJ and Maxx at the dog sitter's, just in case I decided to spend the night. When I pulled into Gypsy's drive, she and Michael were standing out front. Michael looked like she was putting on a little weight.

I guess you can enjoy your food when you aren't dealing with a fool. Stop, Joy.

After I parked, I reached under my car seat and grabbed the weed, but before I got out of the car, Gypsy, dressed in her long sundress, walked up to my car. "Joy, before you come in, Michael is going to spend the night, so I need for you to run to the store and pick up a couple of items." Handing me her list, she said, "I hope you came prepared to spend the night."

Looking at her list, I said, "Damn, girl, we're all on the same page. I just dropped the dogs off on my way over." Handing her the bag of weed, I said, "Take this in the house. No need for me to ride around with it in the car."

As I pulled out of the drive, I looked at the reflection of the two of them in my side mirror, I thought about how much I loved having pajama parties with my girls.

Not to my surprise, before I could leave the store, Gypsy called and asked me to pick up a bag of ice and some ice cream. *Nothing ever changes with these two.*

When I pulled into Gypsy's drive, I could hear the music. After I parked, I called Michael to help me with the bags. When she came out, you could see her smile from across the drive.

Walking into the house, we found Gypsy in the kitchen dancing around like she was at the club. Handing me a drink, she said, "Hey, sis, let's get the party started."

Instead of a cocktail, Michael constantly sipped on a bottle of water she had on the counter.

After I settled in, Michael and I sat on the sofa and chatted while Gypsy was in the kitchen. Looking over at Michael, I told her, "I'm really glad to see you out and about. I know dealing with Darren's death must be hard."

In a matter-of-fact tone, she said, "Joy, after his death, I have uncovered so many of his lies, truths, and deceptions. To be honest, I am not sure if I'm mad about his abuse, or mad at myself for staying so long."

Before she could continue, Gypsy came in. "Ladies, why are you all so quiet?"

Turning to Gypsy, Michael said, "Sorry. I was telling Joy about what I've been feeling about Darren's death. So, ladies, I want to start our party off right. Let me give you all an update of what is and has been going on."

Gypsy walked over and sat on the arm of the sofa. "Okay, baby girl, you have the floor," she said.

In a serious tone, Michael said, "Bear with me—this might take a minute. I must share some of the ugly, the bad, the lovely, and the beautiful of what I've found out after Darren's departure. I have found so many text messages, receipts, and pictures. I'm not going to spoil our time together with the bloody details. However, I will share some of the high points.

"I found Darren's grandmother's will. Per the will for him to receive his trust, he had to be married *and* conceive a baby. I found out he was in a serious relationship with some lady, and from the text and voice messages, they were engaged. He told her he was not sleeping with me so they could have their own baby. So, the night he died, his plan was to tell me he was divorcing me.

"Now, get this. Do you remember when he went to the beach for a meeting, and I was supposed to go, and at the last minute he canceled on me? Well, he took her, and that's where he proposed to her. One thing that broke my heart, her engagement ring looked exactly like the ring Rosie gave me. For a minute, I thought he gave it to her, because you all knew I wasn't able to find it for a long time."

With a quick glance at Gypsy, trying to keep a straight face, I asked, "Did you find your ring?"

With a chuckle, Michael replied, "Yes. Funny, it was in my jewelry box on the dresser. I swore I put that ring in my locked jewelry box."

With a pause, Michael said, "Okay, so I told you the bad. Now let me tell you the ugly. Another message that concerned me was to someone named Karen. He told her his name was Mike, and he was in love with her. From their communication, I honestly think she believed him. Evidently, he did a disappearing move on her, because she left him a voice message a week after his services."

Gypsy and I sat perfectly still with our mouths hanging to the side.

Michael said, "Ladies, close your mouths. Enough of the negative. Let me share the lovely. When they took me to the emergency room, I was given a comprehensive exam. I mean they checked inside and out. Thank God, I didn't have any permanent damage, and I've been going to a therapist to clear, as Joy would say, 'my monkey mind.'"

Gypsy jumped up and screamed, "Group hug!" We sandwiched Michael between the two of us and held her in silence.

Michael broke the silence when she said, "Ladies, I forgot the beautiful."

Excited, Gypsy and I said, "Damn, girl, there's more?"

Michael replied, "Hell yeah, and it is going to change our lives. Well, remember when I told you about the inheritance? The good thing: it will not go to waste."

Gypsy, looking puzzled, said, "I thought you said Darren had to conceive a baby, and if I recall, he stopped sleeping with you."

Smiling, Michael said, "That's correct. The emergency room doctor came back with my test results, and he said all was good, and the baby wasn't harmed."

Gypsy and I looked at her with total shock. I said, "Baby girl, come again?"

With tears running down her face, she replied, "You heard me. I'm having a baby."

We danced around Michael like happy kids. I started to cry, and Gypsy and Michael's faces were also drenched in happy tears. Blowing her nose, Michael said, "Stop with the crying! You all are going to make me have a crying baby."

Gypsy asked, "How in the hell are you pregnant? I thought you said you weren't intimate with Darren."

Laughing, Michael replied, "Who said Darren is the daddy?"

Falling back on the sofa next to Gypsy, I screamed, "Hold the hell up. Who's the daddy?"

Tight-lipped, Michael looked at the both of us like she wasn't going to share her secret. Finally, instead of giving a name, she said, "Let me share my story, and you two geniuses figure it out."

"Gal, get to talking!"

"Well, you remember our PJ party when Darren was on his 'business trip?'"

Gypsy and I replied at the same time, "Yes."

"Well, after everyone left, I went to bed. When I heard Winston start the shower, *What would Darren do?* came to mind."

Gypsy and I replied at the same time again, "What did you do?"

"I wrapped my naked body in the bathrobe Darren's mother gave him for Christmas and strolled upstairs."

Interrupting Michael's story, I asked, "So, what did Michael do?"

"I, uh, I stood at the shower door and watched Winston shower."

Gypsy chimed in, "You did more than watch."

"Yes, I did. I tapped on the shower door, and when Winston opened it, I said, 'Hi, I thought you might need a robe.'"

Through clenched teeth, Gypsy said, "Michael, stop playing and tell it all, I mean blow by blow! The suspense is killing me."

With a shy look, Michael replied, "If you must know, without speaking, he slid my robe off and pulled me into the shower, where I felt my cares wash away. Pressing against the marble walls, we danced to our secret rhythms. Like magic, we embraced ecstasy at the same time. **Before** stepping out of the shower, he put me over his shoulder like a wounded soldier and carried me to bed.

"Ladies, I slept all day after Winston left. When I rolled out of bed, I noticed Darren's robe on the floor. Now, what would Darren do? I picked it up and hung it back in the closet, still damp. I thought, *It will dry before Darren gets home from his extended business trip.*"

Gyspy was speechless, and all I could say was "Well, damn."

With a wink, Michael said, "My mother used to say, find your happy place. You know I am blessed, I found love, joy, and peace in a place that makes me happy."

ACKNOWLEDGMENTS

First, thank you to the Most High for life and for my gift. I hope to make you so proud of me, until the angels born and unborn cry tears of joy.

It's such a blessing to have a new career that you are passionate about. I am thankful for love, being loved, the gift of vision, and the courage to bring my vision to the world. I am honored my ancestors graced me with their presences on more than one occasion on this journey.

Thanks to my first love, Daddy, a wise, loving, and caring soul. Many times in life I brought him my problems and walked away without them. I can still hear him tell me, "Baby, I am your bridge over troubled waters." Damn, I miss him. The only thing he was ever guilty of was spoiling me rotten to the core.

To my mother, whose strength and determination are the wind under my wings, thank you.

To my son, Darrell Sheeley Jr., and daughter-in-law, Danielle Sheeley, thank you for your support and encouragement.

I'm fortunate to have received love from five strong branches on my family tree: the Holmes, Hunts, Hunters, Harrys, and Fraziers. I thank my twin uncles, Albert and

Alfred Hunt, who were my refuge when I got into trouble as a kid, I know you're in Heaven looking down on me. To all of my aunts, uncles, and cousins—on Earth and in Heaven—I love you all.

To my living siblings. I love you both.

To my pets. Their lovely spirits kept me going during my midnight writing sessions.

I have been blessed with wonderful friends. Thanks for being understanding when I had to go into my writer's cave. Special thanks to my big sister-friend, Emma Byrd, who has always supported, encouraged, and believed in me. I appreciate you from the bottom of my soul. You mean the world to me.

Thanks to my goddaughter, Toshia Mae. Stay beautiful.

Dr. M. Wendy Hennequin, my editor, thank you for your patience with me as a first-time author.

Dr. William Harold Hardy, thank you for sharing your experiences and network.

Telma Massie Jackson, the best sister-in-law a girl could ask for, love ya. See ya in the VI.

Thanks to my focus group for your time and honest feedback.

To my cousin, Terrell Dinkins. Your guidance is truly appreciated.

To Ben Walker, thank you for being you and keeping me on track. Yes, I'm still writing.

Thank you to all of the low-vibing spirits and high-energy souls that crossed my path. I continue to grow from both.

Last but not least, I thank each reader for investing your time and hard-earned money supporting my gift. Look out for my next novel. There is more to tell, trust me.

To the world—love 360, see beyond the physical and stay your beautiful selves.

ABOUT THE AUTHOR

BJ Holmes is a creative "free spirit" novelist and a Florida A&M University alumna currently living in metro Atlanta, Georgia. Her mission is to encourage, motivate, and inspire through writing. She is a proud mother of a supportive son and a lovely daughter-in-law.

Determined to turn the COVID-19 lockdown into a positive experience, she used the time alone to complete her first novel. Like the characters in her book, she knows what self-love feels like. She strives to keep moving on her journey, and she trusts that God is with her every step of the way. A nature lover, BJ takes pride in rescuing discarded plants and watching them transform into nature's masterpieces.

For more information about BJ Holmes and her novels, visit www.authorbjholmes.com. Thank you in advance. Stay beautiful.

Made in the USA
Columbia, SC
28 March 2025